THE KNIGHT OF THE ORB

A Legend and a Myth

M.W. PENN

THE KNIGHT OF THE ORB
By M.W. Penn

Published by MathWord Press
Teaching Mathematics through Literature

Copyright © 2017 by M.W. Penn
Cover design by Daphne Firos Peters

ISBN: 978-1-939431-13-4
Library of Congress Control Number: 2017908447

www.mathwordpress.com

For Marie and Bud Torello.

Words are easy, like the wind; faithful friends are hard to find.
WILLIAM SHAKESPEARE

TABLE OF CONTENTS

ENGLAND IN THE REIGN OF KING HENRY III

CHAPTER 1

Robert de Ricwyn Returns to Pynford Castle

The path along the crest of the gentle hill was exposed and he could see to the horizon in all directions. Far ahead, the ochre bulk of Pynford Castle loomed, the steep rocks of its curtain wall shimmering in the summer heat. Behind him, the lush foliage of Pynford Forest faded to a green belt, the reminiscence of a cool, enveloping haven and symbol of a vanishing past; Robert wished he were still riding under its sheltering trees.

Impossible, though. His timeline and his destination were set in stone more immutable than the castle walls; he had no recourse. He rode forward at a slow but steady pace under the punishing summer sun, the only sound the gentle clop of his horse's hooves. The rhythm lulled him into lethargy, the vast openness of the empty countryside into a sense of security. He savored these last moments of solitude; he would arrive at the castle soon enough.

Breaking into this lethargy and into his sense of security, another rider emerged from the forest. A galloping rider. Robert spied him first simply as movement to his rear. A man in the distance, but with a posture—leaning forward, slapping at his horse to encourage speed—that was alarming. He came on at murderous pace, as if intent on overtaking the lone rider.

This did not seem a man Robert wished to meet in a barren spot. He too leaned forward and slapped his own horse, Abatos, into a gallop, creating a wake of dust as he changed pace and charged toward the castle.

And still the unknown rider come on, closing the gap between them. Robert could hear him calling now. He couldn't make out the exact words, but they seemed urgent. The rider wanted him to halt, to turn back.

That would be foolish while alone on the path. The castle was but a short distance away, the protection of a sturdy gate, thick walls and familiar companions suddenly welcoming. If the rider meant no harm, he could approach Robert within the confines of the castle yard. He tightened his grip and slapped Abatos again, and the grey beast flew forward.

Someone up ahead on the castle wall must have been watching Robert's approach and realized his urgency. As Robert came up to the gate, it swung inward on great hinges, opening to him, offering the safety he sought.

He turned as he reached it to see the other rider close behind, his cape flying as he galloped toward the castle wall. His words were clear now. "Halt. Halt. Don't enter the gate. Don't go there." And again an urgent, "Robert de Ricwyn, halt."

Robert did the opposite; he turned away and entered the castle yard at a canter. Once safely inside he ordered the guard to close the gate behind him and make it secure. He dismounted, hot and tired but energized, too, curious about the stranger. A stranger, yes, yet somehow familiar. There was something about the build of the man, his exceptional height in the saddle, the broadness of his chest, the tilt of his head. Could this be someone he knew?

Robert mounted the steps of the curtain wall to the top of its crenelated cap, clearing them two, three at a time. Once above the gate, he ran the wall walk to an embrasure and looked down at the dark figure, retreating now, unwilling to enter the castle walls. This surely was a sign of evil intentions.

And still there was the feeling of familiarity, almost intimacy.

The man halted, turned, as if aware of Robert's gaze. He raised his head and his eyes locked onto Robert's, staring in despair. His demeanor was that of one who suffered a severe loss, who realized that his attempt to secure something valuable to him was now impossible.

Robert was about to call out to the stranger when he,

too, suffered a blow. This man was no stranger. Instead, from high on the sheltering castle wall, Robert stared down into a face that was not only familiar but also a terrifying warning from some distant future.

Sir Robert de Ricwyn was looking at himself.

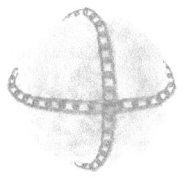

CHAPTER 2
A Tournament Ends in Tragedy

Scheduled as entertainments, tournaments were held to win acclaim and prize money for the knights of a castle and also because they were a good source of revenue for a successful knight's liege lord. Gregory of Pynford held many tournaments at Pynford Castle, forcing Robert to reside at the castle throughout most of the year. After only a brief visit to his family, a visit allowed because Edmund de Ricwyn was failing in health, Robert had returned to Pynford for yet another in their seemingly endless round.

But today the field found Robert distressed. He left his family at a time when he wished to be with them, especially with his elderly mother. Lady Emeline had always held her youngest son close to her heart; it would be a comfort to have him with her as she faced the loss of a protective husband and an uncertain future in the hands of what she felt was a feckless eldest son. Thoughts of his mother, of brothers whose interests often conflicted and of sisters scattered across both lands and loyalties were unsettling him. The specter at the castle wall further disquieted his spirit. He must have been mistaken: it was an effect of the dazzling sunlight off the castle wall, a trick of imagination over fact. But in his heart, he knew it wasn't: he saw what he saw.

Also, much like the day before, this day dawned unfavorably bright and far too warm. Heat was always an enemy when a knight was covered in multiple layers of protection. It intensified the discomfort of being encased in linen underclothing, gambesons and finally heavy mail armor. Even the small cervelliere he wore underneath his great helm became unbearably hot under a bright sun. As his squire lifted the helmet and fitted it over Robert's head and he approached the list for the first joust of the day, Robert felt dizzy and unfocused.

He was to run a first course against Hicket, his best friend from their first days at Pynford. It was only an opening round, a joust to show off the prowess of two of Gregory's most promising young talents. Wedged between the pommel and cantle of his jousting saddle, Robert settled a blunted wooden pole into position and steadied his courser, awaiting the signal to begin.

When the signal came, though, his horse, sensing that Robert was oddly tense, reared and their charge was delayed. To make up for time lost and cover the optimal distance along the list, Robert was forced to increase his normal, steady pace.

But greater speed threw him off. By the time he drew near Hicket and marked the slower cadence of Hicket's horse, Robert was going too fast. Far too fast. Caution screamed into his thoughts: "Don't hit Hicket center at this pace."

Instinctively, he altered course. Slightly. Only slightly. But the shift was exaggerated by his speed.

Hicket, so familiar with the charge of his companion of many years, saw the shift. It was awkward, a movement away from Robert's confident, steady approach. But Hicket couldn't consider consequences, couldn't react. There was no time. The friends who had been through this choreographed combat more times than either could remember now crashed with crushing force. Hicket's pole caught Robert's side as Robert pulled up and away. Robert's shifting pole, forced into an arc by Hicket's blow, caught Hicket's throat under his chin. Unseated by the unexpected hit, Hicket pitched backward and then to the ground as his horse stumbled forward.

Not on him, praise God, but forward. A good thing: many knights were crushed by a falling horse. Yet there was no movement from Hicket's fallen, crumpled body. It was still, still as a corpse. Robert steadied his courser, pushed up from his saddle and ran to his friend.

Robert was awarded a prize for unseating his opponent and allowed to claim his armor even as squires removed Hicket's body from the list. The tournament would go forward as scheduled. But it was over for Robert. He would not mount for another joust, could not bear the heat or the roar of the crowd. His head swam and his stomach turned. He handed his horse over to his squire and followed Hicket's body as other squires carried him to the cool of their quarters. He remained at Hicket's side as the squires removed the armor of both knights.

Hicket was breathing, but his breath was labored, shallow and when a squire attempted to remove his helmet he moaned and writhed in pain. Once the great helm was lifted the reason was clear. The tip of Robert's pole had shattered as it crashed into the metal of Hicket's neck guard, the splintered wood forced up and under the face plate. Blood flowed from a deep gash that cut across his chin, his cheek and into his left eye.

CHAPTER 3
The Making of a Knight

The tournament that brought Robert back to Pynford Castle was meant to be just one more test, another in a series of trials that trained his body but tried his spirit. Each melee and joust brought him ever closer to the life that had been chosen for him, though it was a destiny he would easily forgo.

The goal was set and his quest for knighthood began when he was eight. Eight. A mere child, but a child of Edmund de Ricwyn, lord of modest stretches of land concentrated here in the southwest of England, a holding that included forests for hunting, common pasture land, strips of farming land, a village of cottages for the villeins who worked this land, a stream and water mill, a church and a Manor House.

Sadly, Robert was neither a first son, nor a second. His mother, the lovely Lady Emeline, had given his father three sons and three daughters, all but eliminating Robert's chance of inheriting any of this land or his father's meagre fortune. The cosseted life he led as a young child within the family circle would not be his future; instead he must be trained to make his own way in the world.

More, it could not be the way of his choosing. No child of Ricwyn would be abandoned to his own pursuits; instead, each child would be consigned to a place in society that might in the future bestow further benefits on the family. Daughters forged bonds by marrying into other families; third sons entered the clergy, or, as was the destiny chosen for Robert, they became knights in the household of higher lords.

Knighthood was often a path to increased fortune. Though knights were part of a military order, they belonged to the noble class, and in return for their military service usually received a fief of land from their lord. There were many who sought the advances provided by belonging to this privileged class, but not all soldiers could become knights; those who lacked the expensive equipment, status or family connections were usually denied.

At eight years of age, Robert was sent away from his doting mother, away from the comforts of a crowded nursery and the companionship of a brood of siblings. He was sent here, to Pynford Castle, first as a page, to learn the rules of court—manners, music and poetry—and then the skills of combat. These beginning years were a carefree time in Robert's life as sparring contests were practiced with a close band of friends using wooden swords and shields, often fighting on piggyback to instill the balance that would one day be required in mounted combat.

Later, as he and his companions gained strength and ability and became squires with their training focused more on physical skills—climbing, swimming, throwing stones or javelins, archery, wrestling—Robert found the life was agreeable. He and his fellow squires attended the castle knights, maintained their weapons and witnessed their tactics of fighting on horseback. The pages and squires were also expected to care for the horses in the stable; a knight depended on his horse, so from these early days the bonds between horse and man were forged in both directions.

As the pages grew to manhood, as ballads and wooden swords gave way to padded armor and sharpened steel, Robert de Ricwyn excelled. The two-handed sword, battle axe, mace and dagger—the weapons of knighthood—were suited to his superior height and strength. But it was his horsemanship that became a source of envy, not only among his fellow pages, but among the older knights of the castle, too.

Robert seemed to understand almost instinctively that horses were the most important component in the life of a knight. A well-equipped knight would own several horses with each serving a different purpose and ranging in size from a palfrey or an ambler, used for general travelling purposes, to a big, powerful warhorse.

Warhorses were strong enough to carry a knight and armor into battle, but also agile enough to play a part in tournaments and jousts. Most often stallions bred and raised from foals specifically for the needs of war, they had powerful hindquarters and were able to coil and spring; stop, spin and turn; or carry their armored burden in a sprint forward. The best warhorses were heavily muscled, with strong bones and a well-arched neck. Commonly called destriers, the greatest of these horses were known as coursers. Because of his recognized ability, Robert's family agreed to equip him with the finest courser available.

A knight of great size and skill astride a fine courser was a valuable asset to the castle of Pynford, so Gregory, Lord of Pynford and Robert's liege lord, set Robert to jousting with a quintain at a young age. A shielded dummy suspended from a swinging pole, the quintain when hit accurately by a charging knight would move to the side; if hit off center, though, it could rotate full circle to knock the rider from the saddle. In little time, Robert became deft at hitting the center of the quintain, spinning it to its full 360° with one forceful blow of his lance, and then quickly avoiding its spinning arm. The 'couch'— riding forward on horseback with a lance held securely under one arm to steady it during a course and increase its thrust and accuracy in a lunge—became Robert's trademark. While still considered a youth, he became its unrivaled champion. Riding the course was a common part of tournaments. Before other squires his age were considered for knighthood, Gregory bestowed the honor of riding the course on Robert, so that he could compete in tournaments. Galloping across a field toward another mounted and armored rival and aiming a long, blunt pole at his shield to unseat him became Robert's trademark.

Though the poles were not sharpened lances and the combatants wore armor, riding the course was not without danger. Knights always feared falling from a galloping destrier; broken bones ended careers. Among Pynford's many promising young squires, only Hicket could withstand a blow from Robert's charge. But not every time.

CHAPTER 4
The Scullery Maid

As Mila poured water from the cauldron into the sink, it steamed up into her face. Heat rose from nearby fires, curled in smoke and flew outward with the sizzling grease of the spit. The metal pot was hot, and now the stone basin was hot. She was hot. Hot and tired. Her shoulders ached. Noise from the crowd at her back, from their pounding and grinding and calling orders, buzzed in her ears.

Heat and noise and aching bones was the daily life she endured since the time she was old enough to work in the kitchen—tall enough to reach the stone sink, strong enough to lift the cauldron from the fire. And there was nothing else. Mila had no other past she could remember and saw no other future. At least the midday meal was in the past, most of the debris cleared, remains given over to the servants, trenchers thrown to the dogs. Once this lot was scrubbed she might steal a bit of time to rest in the yard.

Suddenly, the voice of a hall servant rose above the

normal clamor and the kitchen grew silent. Mila set down the cauldron and listened: two Knights and their squires had arrived after riding hard all the way from distant York and, adhering to the customary generosity of Pynford Castle, they would be fed and offered lodging in the hall.

The stillness in the room behind her remained for just a heartbeat and then the buzz returned at a higher pitch. Someone was calling new orders: "A cheese tart, stuffed eggs, crispels." Mila turned from her task to see rich beef frumenty ladled into a bowl by another girl about her own age. Her own age, yes, but taller and with golden hair.

Mila's hair wasn't golden, nor was it dark; instead, it had the same nothing color as the dirty water in the stone sink. Her eyes were a good match for it, too, not deep green or dark brown or bright blue, not much of anything. Her face was thin, her features sharp. Over time Mila had come to realize that the one thing she was was forgettable.

Dispensable, too. If she weren't here to carry the water and scrub the pots, someone else would take her place. Who would miss her? The boys who carried in wood all stopped to talk to the girl with the golden hair. The quiet youth that swept and brought fresh rushes for the floor sometimes had a pleasant word for Mila, but mostly he was just polite when he asked her to move out of his way.

As she worked, Mila's thoughts drifted to Robert de Ricwyn the tall, dark Robert who was the most handsome young knight of Pynford: Robert in the stable with his black hair tumbling across his forehead; Robert atop a huge courser jousting in the yard; Robert in armor at a tournament. She had watched him whenever she had the chance for so many years now—for the many she could remember. He was older than her, but not by many summers. Still, he would be knighted now. Then, most likely he would be sent off to—where?

Mila had no idea of places beyond the walls of Pynford.

When the last of her chores were done for the day, she could finally escape the heat and noise of the kitchen. But beef frumenty wasn't the food of her ilk. She took her bowl from its shelf, ladled a portion of porridge into it and, when no one was watching, slipped away into a far corner of the kitchen garden, a corner well hidden behind the tall feathery green tops of a patch of carrots. It was her private spot at this time of the year when the vegetables grew tall and her small, dull frame would disappear into the shadows.

Happily, this wall bordered the courtyard of the squires and knights of the castle. If it was quiet, as it often was at this hour when evening set in, Mila could hear sounds on the other side. Now the first sound she heard was someone speaking.

It was the injured Hicket. Mila was certain that was his voice.

"Poor Hicket" he was called now. Those in the kitchen who understood these matters were saddened by his circumstance. He was skilled, courteous and well liked among all the other squires, both the younger boys and those about to receive knighthoods; but since he had lost the sight of one eye he could never be considered for dubbing. What would become of him?

When she first learned that his injury would keep him from becoming a knight, she daydreamed that he might instead come to work in the kitchens. Then one day, Sir Robert would surely come by to visit his old companion and Mila would meet the handsome knight, source of so many of her daydreams.

But now the next voice she heard was Robert's. He was with Hicket on the other side of the wall. They were talking about something important. She could hear it in their tone. Hidden by the gathering dusk, she crept from her corner to get closer to the voices, kneeling now to be nearer to the top of the wall.

"What will become of you then? We must find a better course than that for you."

"Robert, it is not for you to decide. You have no responsibility in this."

She heard the forgiveness in Hicket's voice, forgiveness and perhaps frustration, too; but Mila couldn't see Robert's grim face as he turned away from his friend.

CHAPTER 5
Robert is Summoned to Ricwyn

The days following the joust blurred in Robert's memory. Heat stilled many of the usual activities in the knights' quarter and even the horses in the stable sank into lethargy.

Robert stayed with Hicket, watching as monks and herbalists tended his wound, listening as they whispered dire prognostications. Miraculously, though, the gash didn't fester and the edges began to heal. Within a short time it was evident that Hicket would survive, that the end result of the combat would be no worse than an ugly scar across his pale, handsome face. And that his left eye was lost to him.

Robert was never certain about when Hicket became aware of the loss. He gained consciousness, endured the ministrations of the monks, began to eat and drink, grew stronger. Together, they spoke of the heat, of the uncommon stillness in the stable yard, even of the monks—mocking the credit the good men took for the wonders of their herbs and poultices. But Hicket never mentioned the injury that now altered his future, never said, "This wound has taken the purpose of my life from me."

Hicket was from a peasant family attached to Pynford castle, his father merely a vassal of Lord Gregory, and Hicket was grateful for his chance of a knighthood. Though never quite as strong or proficient as Robert, from their youth Hicket was determined to be the better knight. Throughout their years together, he trained harder, longer. He volunteered for unpopular duties and entered competitions with an impassioned fire that Robert lacked. He loved the sport of it and he loved the glory. More, he often spoke of his family and of the benefits his knighthood would bring to them.

And Robert had shattered this dream with one blow of a blunted pole. The senselessness of shattering the life his friend had worked toward for so many years haunted him—would haunt him forever. But not once did Hicket accuse him.

As they did often in the evenings since Hicket was able to walk, they were sitting together in the stable yard sharing a pitcher of ale, enjoying the slanted rays of a setting sun and avoiding the unpleasant truth of the inevitable course of futures that soon must diverge onto separate paths—one into knighthood and further glory, one into nothingness—when a rider trotted through the inner gate bringing news. Robert had awaited a messenger since he was forced to leave his family, expecting each day to hear that his father Edmund de Ricwyn had died and his eldest brother, Balian de Ricwyn, was now lord of the family estates.

But the news this rider brought was even more distressful. "Robert de Ricwyn?" the mounted figure addressed both young men with the question. His eyes were immediately drawn to the disfiguring slash across Hicket's face and he tried to disguise his repulsion by looking away, steadying his horse and then dismounting.

"Aye." Robert stood to face the rider who gladly focused on the unmarred face.

"I have brought a message from the Lord Balian de Ricwyn."

"My brother," Robert stated it as a matter of fact. So his brother was 'Lord Balian de Ricwyn'. It had happened. "Yes, my lord." The man looked down now, as if reluctant to begin.

"The message?" Robert was impatient to get through this.

The man raised his eyes. "It is in two parts, my lord. First, I bring news that your father has died."

Robert looked into the eyes of the stranger and held them for an instant. The man seemed honestly grieved to bring him this news.

Hicket stood now, came to Robert's side and lifted his arm to Robert's shoulder. Robert turned to acknowledge his friend's support as the rider, still uncomfortable, avoided looking at Hicket.

"And the other..." Robert prompted him.

"Lord Balian sends your brother Roland to Ireland, my lord. He is to assist the Welsh at Wexford, sir, those who plan to expand their territories in that land."

Robert's eyes narrowed. So Balian was wasting no time. Never content with life as the eldest son of a lesser family, he would attempt to increase his influence by any means possible. Balian must feel that Wexford offered such an opportunity and that the clever Roland might find a way to expand the family holdings there. Still, if the mission involved combat, the quiet steward, Roland, would not be a good choice.

And it must involve combat. Years ago, at the time when England was ruled by the Norman King Henry II, Dermot MacMurrough, the exiled Irish King of Lienster, had encouraged a Norman ally to invade Wexford, a town at the south eastern tip of Ireland, and to subdue the native tribes of the surrounding country side. Lesser barons from Wales contributed archers and cavalry to the endeavor and then recruited Irishmen loyal to King MacMurrough to swell their army further. When the Welsh armies forced the Viking city of Wexford to submit to the rule of the exiled King MacMurrough, the king gave Wexford and the surrounding area to these lesser Welsh barons as payment for their help.

The expansion of English and French control in Ireland that began under Henry II continued to the present. The response of the Irish Kings was largely to submit to the more powerful invaders. It was the native people of Ireland, the lords of small manors, who were often unhappy with this foreign force in their lives.

Much of the island remained in upheaval as forced land exchanges between native and invader resulted in constantly shifting frontiers. Still, a stable colony might be established by subduing the Irish population, building fortress castles and founding English-Norman towns. This was a path that could lead to extending land holdings for the invaders, a path that would be supported by the English monarchy and, as such, one that provided an opportunity for men like Balian de Ricwyn.

"Balian moves so soon?" Robert didn't realize he had spoken his thought until the rider quickly brought his thoughtful gaze to meet Robert's again. They stared into each other's eyes for a brief moment.

Hicket broke the tense silence. "I know you grieve for the loss of your father, Robert. This should not be a time to consider other matters."

"Aye," Robert agreed. He again addressed the rider. "My mother, the Lady Emeline? She is well?"

"Aggrieved in spirit, my lord, but in good health."

"Thank you for riding the distance to bring this message. You will no doubt be a guest of this house until you are ready to return." Robert's tone was of dismissal. He turned toward Hicket.

"My lord." The man obviously had more to say. Robert

turned to him again. "Lord Balian wishes you to return to Ricwyn, my lord. He has sent me to request of Lord Gregory that you will be allowed to return to your family until such time as Lord Roland returns from his mission to Ireland."

"Until Roland returns from Ireland? But that could be months. Years." A scowl tightened Robert's chiseled features. Then a second, even more unpleasant thought hardened them. "You must speak with my liege lord. That may not be possible."

"Indeed, Lord Balian has charged me to offer incentives to Gregory."

Robert again stared into the rider's eyes and moments passed.

It was again Hicket who broke the tension that seemed to escalate between the other two. "Well, now is not the time," he said. "That can be discussed on the new day." Robert looked at his friend and understood the wisdom of his caution. "Hicket is right. Go now. The entrance to the hall is beyond that gate. Leave your horse here; we will have it tended."

The man wanted to say more, but Robert was having none of it. He took Hicket's arm and guided him back to the bench, leaving the bringer of such unwanted news on his own. The man handed the reins of his tired horse to an approaching squire and left the courtyard.

The friends sat quietly in the warmth of the setting sun, Robert reviewing in his mind the words of the rider, but Hicket knew his friend well. After a time he broke into Robert's pensive silence. "The news of your father has saddened you Robert. I grieve, too, at your loss. But there is more troubling you."

"Return to Ricwyn!" he scowled. "It is not something I wish to do."

"But surely the Lady Emeline would welcome a visit. You speak often of her and worry about her wellbeing."

"If that were the purpose of my return, I would welcome it; but that is not Balian's intention."

"You fear he has other intentions?"

"I fear he has no intention of sending Roland off on a mission to Ireland on his own. The land there is restless and Roland is no fighter."

Robert leaned back, rested his broad shoulders against the warm stone of the courtyard wall, lowered his head and closed his eyes, forcing Hicket to follow his thoughts. At last, coming to the same conclusion as Robert, he was astounded. "Surely not!" And then, "But you are pledged here, Robert. Gregory is your liege lord. You cannot leave here to pursue a family adventure in Ireland."

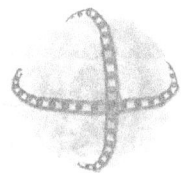

CHAPTER 6
Mila Discovers a Plot

Mila moved along the path quietly to huddle against the back wall of the kitchen garden, the place she escaped to whenever she could. She realized that since the accident Robert and Hicket were often in the knights courtyard at this time of evening, and if she were very still she could hear them talking. "Surely not!" It was Hicket's voice. And then, "But you are pledged here, Robert. Gregory is your liege lord."

Now she was astonished. What was that Hicket said now? "You cannot leave here to pursue a family adventure in Ireland." 'You cannot leave here.' She stood to listen.

"I know my brother, Hicket. He has waited for this day, longed for it."

"It is the way, Robert. You knew Balian would be the next lord of Ricwyn after your father. It is only as expected."

"Balian is least worthy. He was a greedy child; he will

be a greedy lord. And harsh. I fear for my mother. He will not treat her well."

"Still, there is no recourse. But Ireland? You seem most concerned with his plan in this, Robert."

"I am. He sends Roland, Hicket, and that makes no sense. Roland is a gentle soul, a scholar, a clerk. He is the steward who manages the Ricwyn finances. He tends to income from the lands and to the taxes, he should not be sent on this mission. What reason would Balian have for making this choice?"

They fell silent for a time and Mila pressed closer to the wall.

"Might Balian have reason to want Roland out of the way?" Hicket asked.

"That seems a more reasonable answer. But if that is the case, why send for me? I might also interfere with any disagreeable plans Balian has made. Why not allow me to remain here at Pynford?"

Hicket thought for a moment. "Pynford is not far from the major Ricwyn landholding, Robert. Perhaps Balian worries that soon you will be a respected knight and may even earn your own holding. Perhaps you are too close?"

"If that is true, then Balian has less reason to keep me with him." Robert fell silent, pondering his brother's intent. "No, if that is true, then I would be far better out of his way—out of his way much as Roland will be out of his way."

"You mean in Ireland?"

"It would make more sense to send a knight over a

clerk."

Hicket considered this. "Together they would make a strong combination. Any force sent to Wexford could only benefit from the ability of a fighting knight and the organization of a worthy steward."

"The steward and the knight might also forge a strong alliance to each other," Robert said, thoughtfully. "Among all my brothers and sisters, I would choose Roland as the best. Balian must know this. Why would he band us together?"

Both fell silent now. At last Hicket said, "We ponder all these questions, Robert, and still we are not certain that Balian intends to send you to Wexford with Roland."

"But he does. I am sure of it. And more, I will not go."

"Not go? Robert, if Balian has settled on this plan, then you must. Once you return to Ricwyn, you cannot refuse him."

"Then I will not return."

"And if Lord Gregory sends you? If our conjectures are near to the true intentions of Balian, then he has most assuredly provided good reason for Gregory to comply with his request."

"He may ask Gregory to be part of this plot, Hicket. The Lord of Pynford never fails to seek benefit from missions of the type Balian has planned in Wexford." Robert considered this. "But no, if that were the case, Balian's force would be dwarfed by the force Gregory could assemble. The mission would become Gregory's and so the gains would be his. No, I fear that Balian will devise another reason for asking Gregory to allow me to return to Ricwyn, and it will not be the truth."

"Then you are double doomed, Robert. Still, you have no recourse in the matter."

"I agree. If I am here, I have no recourse."

"And you are here."

"I am here today, Hicket."

Hicket's response was immediate. "What are you saying, Robert?" Mila heard the doubt, or perhaps it was fear, in his voice.

"Where will you be tomorrow, Hicket?"

Hicket shrugged, but Mila couldn't see that. She only heard Robert's response to the gesture.

"It seems we have both lost our intended futures."

Hicket protested. "No. You will be a famous knight, Robert. A great knight, well respected. You will have your own demesne one day."

"I have no heart for knighthood. Certainly not the heart that you have always had. I never had your intense desire, my friend."

"But what else can you do?"

"I can leave."

"Leave? Leave Pynford? And go where?"

Robert was silent.

"Where, Robert?"

"Well, first to Ricwyn." He paused. "But not to Balian. To my mother. And then perhaps to Roland. After I determine what plans Balian has formed, I can choose my own course."

"So you will leave me, Robert." Hicket's voice held a sadness that Mila, too, understood. "I knew we must part, but this has come too soon. You have been my friend for a long time."

"Part? Hicket, why should we part? No, you must come with me."

"With you?"

"You have no other plans."

Hicket considered for a moment then made a thoughtful response. "I am but a burden to Gregory and will be a burden to my family if I return to them. So, yes, I have no plans."

"You will never be a burden, Hicket. You are young and strong."

Both were silent for a time and Mila held her breath, waiting. "And when are you planning this escape, Robert?" "It must not wait. So tomorrow. In the early hours, long before we will be missed. We will leave soon after they open the gates."

"Tomorrow? Robert, I have no horse. My courser belongs to Gregory."

"I have two horses. My palfrey will serve for the journey."

"You speak of this as if it were something we might accomplish." Hicket sounded amazed.

"It is something we must do. I feel I have no other

choice."

"It is I with few choices before me, Robert. In truth, this is the best I might imagine."

"Tomorrow, then, soon after the gates open."

"Tomorrow, then."

Mila didn't see them clasp each other by the arm, but she imagined them sealing their pact with some gesture.

She sank down beside the wall. Tomorrow. Tomorrow!

She didn't even consider her action or any of its consequences. Her only thought was that she must prepare for the journey. She was leaving Pynford tomorrow when the gates opened. The night ahead was all the time she had to make ready.

CHAPTER 7
A Thief in the Night

Food. Food and something to carry it in. And she must find a better cloak; she had always wanted a good cloak and now she would have one. A horse would be impossible, but she was small and light and Robert's courser was massive; yes, she could ride behind Robert.

She left her bowl where it rested at the base of the wall and turned to leave the garden.

"Wait, the carrots," she thought. She returned and pulled four from the soft earth, frowned—and pulled six more. She twisted off their feathery tops and threw the carrots into the bowl which would serve to hold them while she returned to the kitchen. As she crept along the garden wall she added several fat onions and beets to the mix.

The kitchens were never idle; someone was always grinding or roasting or sweeping. But Mila's small, quiet presence was familiar to everyone and no one would pay her any heed. She hid her bowl of vegetables near the edge of the garden, marking the spot in her mind, and slipped into the dim space, first returning to the sink to stand in her usual place. After a few moments she turned and surveyed the room. The golden haired girl worked at the central table bent over a mortar; one of the old men who tended the spit sat on a stool by his fire, almost asleep; a saucier stirred a pot that swung over another, lower fire. All seemed preoccupied with their tasks or their own thoughts.

Mila walked by the golden haired girl who concentrated on the nuts she was grinding, passing at her back. Freshly made sausages hung above a bench by the open door. Seizing her chance, Mila slipped two rings from the hook, tossed them into a blackened pot and was out the door before anyone noticed. She added the vegetables from her bowl in the garden to the pot.

A cloak was her next aim, and that would be more difficult. She would have to enter the great hall for that, but it was already dark and the massive door at the front would be bolted now. She would have to go through the kitchens—again. This was pushing her luck. She knew it, but there was no other way.

She returned to the kitchen, but not to her sink. Instead she stole silently along the edge of the room to the back corner. She was in plain sight of the fair haired girl now and the girl lifted her head to frown at Mila, but she didn't say anything. She added more nuts to the mortar bowl and pressed on with her task. Just then one of the boys who brought wood came in from the yard carrying a huge bundle of logs. He took them to the fire where the saucier worked.

"Put them down,' the man said grumpily. "I don't want this fire to blaze yet."

The boy dropped the wood with a clatter and several logs rolled across the floor.

"Now look what you've done." The saucier grabbed a log that rolled to his feet and swiped at the boy. "Gather them up. Stack them over there."

Everyone turned to watch the boy hunch under the severe blow across his shoulders and quickly bend to his task. Everyone but Mila, who slipped through the passage into the hall.

The fire at the center of the great chamber burned low in the heat of the evening and the hall was dim. People were settling down for the night hours. Soon, most would be asleep. Mila crept along the wall to a dim corner far from the fire and waited her chance. She was too agitated to sleep, too uncomfortably wedged in the angle of roughly chiseled stone walls and the damp stone floor. Her body cramped as the evening chill set in, but she was still too afraid to move. Her greatest advantage would be that she remained unnoticed.

Hours passed. She thought the hall would never settle. It never did, completely, but after a time, this corner had grown quiet, the heavy breathing of sleep the only sound.

She gathered all her courage. It was time. She wouldn't stand; too much risk in that. Catlike and as silently as possible, she emerged from her shadowy corner and crept among those making a bed of the hall floor.

Travelers of lower rank, hall servants? She had no idea who most were, but she knew what she wanted from one of them. Slowly, attentive to all the sounds around her, she worked her way across the room. At the far end was the separate chamber of the lord and lady and their servants. Near this door the caliber of the cloth in robes and cloaks scattered on straw mats improved markedly. She couldn't see their color in the dark, but she felt softness and little wear.

One cloak, thrown to the side because of the summer warmth, was of the finest cloth she had ever felt. More, on the reverse side was another layer of cloth, a soft layer that shown bright even in the dimness. Mila thought it must be made of clouds. Slowly she began to gather the cloak toward her, winding it into a ball as she worked. Once, twice a sleeper behind her stirred and she froze. As he settled, she continued. Carefully, carefully. Soon the cloak was a small bundle at her chest. She tucked it under her arm and began to creep backward along the route she had come.

Suddenly her foot slid into something that scraped on the stone floor. She was moving slowly, so it didn't move a great distance, but it did make a noise. She froze again, waiting. A stirring, then heavy breathing and stillness. She changed course slightly, shifting around the object, whatever it was. As she wormed backward toward the kitchen passage, the object became visible as a dark block resting on the floor: a box of some kind. Not too big, it was the size of some kitchen safe boxes used to hold precious spices. Mila ran her fingers over the surface; it was ornately carved, a certain sign of precious contents. Spices or perhaps healing herbs. These could be useful on the journey.

She was near the kitchen passage now. Might she dare it? Rising to a crouch, she lifted the box. It wasn't spices. It was far too heavy.

"Leave it," she thought. But how? Now that she held the box and the cloak, too, setting the heavy box down on the stone floor with one hand would make a clatter. She was reluctant to release her hold on the precious cloak. She would have to take both.

Crouching now, carrying her spoils, she made her way toward the kitchen passage as quickly as possible. As she slipped in she was relieved to find that both fires had died down and the room was dim. The girl with the golden hair and the saucier were gone; only the man who tended the spit and the boy who brought wood were there. Each was half asleep and neither noticed her. She stole quietly through the kitchen and back into the garden.

The pot was just where she left it. Now her only task was to secure something to wrap the cloak, the food, and the heavy box. Her old cloak might do; it was threadbare and of such a dull color that it would never draw attention. But it would have to be done quietly. Then she would have to find a place near the main gate where she could hide until they opened it in the morning. All this would take time.

The hoot of an owl startled her. Mila froze again, waiting. Silence. She slipped behind a cask and surveyed the garden and the stone court that surrounded the kitchen door, looking for signs of life. She found the owl perched at the top of a gate that separated the kitchens from the main courtyard. It seemed to peer straight at her, then turned away to look into the other yard, its head rotating 180° in the peculiar manner of owls.

Suddenly the huge spotted bird hooted and flew upward in a flurry. In a moment there was a sharp sound on the other side of the gate and it pushed inward. Mila crouched, slipped further into the garden, watched. It was one of the cooks, coming to begin work on the meals for the next day. The man headed straight to the kitchen door leaving her alone in the garden. But it was a warning. The summer dawn was not far away.

By the time the Pynford gate opened to admit the peasants from the castle's village, the servants and workers who entered the castle grounds each morning to do the menial work of running the household, Mila was in place. As the workers, varied in age and gender but consistently drab, streamed through the wide gate, she joined them. Then, unnoticed, she slipped backward and out through the wall that had provided her a home and protection for as long as she had memories.

The huts of the peasants clustered at the back of the castle wall, on the slope of a hill. Their fields lay beyond the huts, on the far side of a swift stream that flowed through the bottom of a rocky gully; the gully and stream offered both the small settlement and the castle protection from enemies.

But on this gated side a gentle, downward slope held nothing but an open, barren landscape, a landscape kept bare to better defend the gate. There was nothing to conceal an approach from watchful eyes at the top of the castle wall. On the horizon, the green belt of Pynford Forest was just visible, but it would take Mila a good part of the morning to walk there.

Though shelter from watchful eyes was the first problem she faced, the second was even more difficult. When Robert and Hicket left the castle, what direction would they take? There was a straight, broad path along what seemed a direct line from the castle to the forest; surely this was the route horsemen rode. But another path worn into the earth trailed off to her left and disappeared around the corner of the crenelated castle wall.

Mila wished she could just wait near the gate, but this was fraught with the danger of the gatekeeper noticing her when the crowd of peasants thinned. She had no better choice. Hoping no one would pay heed to a lone peasant moving away from the castle gates, and hoping, too, that Robert and Hicket would indeed follow the road toward Pynford forest, Mila shouldered her bundle and walked that way.

CHAPTER 8
Danger on the Forest Path

It would be best to leave early, before Gregory could send the messenger to Robert to repeat the orders to return to Ricwyn. Ignoring the sleeping squires, Hicket and Robert tended to Robert's horses themselves, preparing the smaller black Luagor and the huge, grey Abatos for the journey.

Luagor would carry Hicket and the small packets of provisions they managed to gather. Abatos bore the heavier burden; the courser had grown comfortable carrying the weight of Robert and his armor into a joust and would now have to bear both on their journey. Hicket's squire came into the stable as they were securing Robert's armor to Abatos.

The squire was startled by their preparations, but understood when Robert explained the message sent from his brother asking him to return to Ricwyn. Since Robert failed to mention his intention not to return, there was no immediate reason to further question his sudden departure. It also seemed right to the squire that Hicket would go with his friend, and he left them to their task. The summer sun was barely above the horizon and the castle dwellers just coming to life as they rode through the stable yard to the castle gate and trotted down the path that led to Pynford Forest.

Mila turned at the sound of approaching hoof beats, relieved to see Robert and Hicket bearing down on her. It was too soon, though; they were only a short distance from the castle gate, still in view of the guards. She hesitated, but in the end had no recourse; if she didn't stop them now, they would ride away and she would have no chance of ever catching up with travelers on horseback.

She raised her hand in a gesture to stop them. Hicket was the first to slow and turn his horse to face her. Soon Robert, who had ridden on ahead, also turned and came back to his friend.

"Please, my lord," Mila asked in a most plaintive voice, "may I beg a ride?"

Robert appraised Mila, stringy hair and ragged tunic, shook his head at Hicket, and turned Abatos toward the forest again. But Hicket hesitated.

"It promises to be another hot day, Robert. The sun will soon beat down on this barren path. We might give the child a ride into the cool shade of the forest. It will ease her journey."

Robert only nodded. He knew his friend well, knew that

Hicket would feel concern for this unfortunate peasant burdened with a huge, heavy sack and walking under a hot sun.

"Quickly, then, Hicket. We must be off."

Hicket leaned down toward Mila, offering her his arm, and she swung up into the saddle behind him.

"Thank you, my lord," was all she could murmur. In truth she was stunned. In her world, the odds against this happening were enormous. And yet, it was just as she had planned. She smiled into Hicket's back as he turned his horse and they rode down the path together.

"Now try to get rid of me," she thought. And, as they entered the shaded path of Pynford Forest, they didn't.

Robert, pondering the consequences of their sudden departure and, more, fearing what awaited him at the manor of Ricwyn, had all but forgotten the spare, scrubby peasant girl. Hicket was aware of her presence but willing to allow her to ride with them as long as possible.

The three riders were already deep into the forest, moving along the heavily shaded path at a steady pace, when it happened: a scruffy band of thieves leapt from the bushes on the trail, suddenly encircling both horses closing in both in front and to the rear, blocking their escape.

One stepped forward and ordered, "Dismount!"

The riders only hesitated.

"Dismount, I say." The band of scraggly men drew closer around the horses. "Now!" The speaker leapt toward Abatos and grabbed for his reins.

"No!" Mila's voice rang shrill, piercing through Hicket's ear: shrill, strong and full of authority.

Her gaze took in all of the men on the ground, but it was the ruffian still trying to grab the reins from Robert who turned and lunged toward her.

"No?" He stared at her with red, wild eyes. "Who is it that gives orders here?" He grabbed for her foot, but she kicked forward with such force she knocked him backward into the men behind.

Stunned silence gave her a moment to think. Alas, she couldn't think of a thing.

It was Abatos who reacted with swift authority. Trained for combat, he allowed no one to challenge his knight. Ragged attackers on foot were as threatening as armored men on horseback. He rose onto his strong back haunches, sending his front hooves flying high above the heads of the men still in front of him and then crashing down on the head of the man closest to him, sending him to the ground. Abatos reared again, this time pivoting, snorting hot breath, coming down on another head.

Knives appeared from under cloaks and men lunged at Luagor ready to slash at Mila and Hicket. But now Mila had had time to react. The bundle she carried was heavily weighted by the iron pot and the odd carved box. She grabbed it and swung downward with all her might and another man fell, bleeding.

Hicket held his own dagger now, slashing left and

right. It was a scene of flashing hooves and daggers, makeshift clubs and piercing screams—chaos that at this point could shift either way.

But for the man in the dark cloak.

He was a massive rider on a dark courser every bit the size of Abatos. In the midst of the clamber, no one remembered seeing him approach; he simply appeared on the path in front of Robert and the rearing Abatos. When his horse, too, suddenly reared and its massive hooves tore the air above the heads of the thieves, the fight was over. The band of men melted into the forest just a quickly and quietly as they had appeared, leaving three of their number behind on the ground.

Robert spun toward his friend. "Hicket?"

"I'm well, Robert. Scratches only." Hicket turned to Mila and then bent to inspect the sides and legs of Luagor. "No serious damage that I can see."

Robert looked into Mila's eyes, but was at a loss for words. Her shrill cry had given them that one brief moment they needed. He nodded to her then leaned forward to stroke the neck of Abatos, to calm him and show his gratitude.

By the time he looked back to the man who appeared on the path, the stranger had his back to them and was riding away at a trot.

Hicket pulled Luagor aside Abatos and began to call out to the stranger. "Wait, wait. We must thank you for...."

But Robert put his hand on Hicket's arm. "Let him go,

Hicket. He must know that he saved us."

"But we should reward him, Robert. We should in the least....'

"No, Hicket. I believe he chose not to speak to us."

Hicket's one good eye narrowed into a frown. Robert was one to always repay a debt. "But why? Do you know this man?"

Instead of answering, Robert surveyed the ground around them. "We must move on quickly. We shouldn't remain here and allow the band time to regroup. I fear they have much to repay us for."

And Robert de Ricwyn didn't hesitate. He gathered the reins close, guiding Abatos forward through the carnage, following in the footsteps of a dark stranger who was himself.

CHAPTER 9
A Band of Three

Robert and Hicket were reluctant to slow their pace while in the confines of the forest, and Mila willingly agreed—though no one asked her opinion. The three riders moved forward at a fast pace, the bright sun at times splintering through overhanging branches to blind them only to disappear again into the thick blanket of leaves, as it shifted steadily eastward in the sky.

Then suddenly, just as abruptly as it had enveloped them, Pynford Forest released them, spilling them into the brightness of another barren plain. Blazing sun stunned Mila out of the lethargy that had settled in as she clung to Hicket and rested her head against his back, the steady rhythm of horses' hooves thrumming a soothing lullaby.

Robert slowed Abatos and Hicket pulled Luagor astride.

"Ricwyn, Robert? How far is it?"
"Not far now. I have never made this journey in such good

time." He frowned at the thought of the unusual shortness of time, but quickly forgot it as he considered their arrival and all it would entail. "The village fields begin but a few hours ride ahead. The manor house is on a rise at the far side of the village with the manse's hunting grounds spreading behind it." Then he had another concern. He pulled Abatos to a halt and gazed at his friend, wan and weakened from weeks of recovery. "Are you growing weary, Hicket?"

"I would like to rest for a time, if we might."

"Of course. We will stop here." Mila was grateful for the respite until Robert turned his attention to her. "And what of you? Where do you go from here?"

Well, she really wasn't going to anywhere, was she? Only away, and only with them. She lowered her head to think, and Robert grew suspicious.

"You are running from Pynford." He said it as a matter of fact.

And what would he do to a runaway? Mila looked up into his stern face but no words came from her.

Hicket's gentle voice calmed her. "Have you run away, child?" But still she had no answer. "Have you?"

"Not really. I mean, I'm not bound to Pynford."

"Why were you there? What was your place?"

"I worked in the kitchens, my lord. I scrubbed the pots."

It was Robert who considered the status of her servitude. "For how long?"

"For the turning of many seasons, my lord. For as long

as I can remember."

Hicket's brow furrowed. "But you are still a child."

"And you say you are not bound?" Robert, too, was incredulous.

"But I am not."

"How did you come to Pynford?" Hicket asked.

"I was just there, sire. No one seems to remember when I came, or from where. At least no one will say."

An abandoned child, Hicket thought. A common thing. For all of Gregory's love of war and jousting, the household of Pynford was a gentle haven for its time. Instead of abandoning an unwanted babe, the servants would be encouraged to nurse her, then put her to use in the kitchen for her keep.

"But why did you leave?" Hicket asked.

Again Mila struggled to explain. "I knew it was time, sire."

"Time?" Robert believed none of it. "Or was there another reason? What have you done that would deserve punishment?"

"I have done nothing. I did my tasks well and was almost never scolded."

"So you left for no reason and you are going nowhere?" Robert was not convinced. Mila could only lower her eyes and further convince him of her guilt.

Hicket, who had studied her chapped red hands as she held on to him during the ride, knew that her work must have taken a heavy toll on the girl. "You must tell us the truth. We must feel we can trust you, or..."

"Or?" She hugged him closer to her. "Oh, you will abandon me here. Please, I have nowhere to go."

"The truth, then," he insisted.

She hesitated and he shifted and reached for the bundle she had attached to his belongings.

"Wait, I will tell you." And her story spilled out through streaming tears. "You see, I heard you make your plans. I was at the garden wall last evening and heard you."

"You were listening?"

"I had no thought to listen, not at first. I often rest at the back of the garden. I take my dinner there on hot days." She stopped.

"And?" Hicket insisted.

"I heard you talking in the stable yard and I knew then that I wanted to leave Pynford just as you did."

"So you slipped away and followed us." Robert was annoyed.

"I slipped away. I was away at first light."

Hicket saw the reasonableness of this. "Robert, we can both attest that she wasn't following us. We came across her on the path."

"Yes," Mila agreed. "You see, I felt that if you could find the courage to leave Pynford, then I could. So I did. Nothing more." Of course it had been her plan to go with them, but then she was forced to go ahead; so this might be true or not.

"Nothing more?" Robert was still not a believer of her

tale.

She gathered courage from Hicket's broad smile. "But we are clear of the forest. It is time we should rest and eat."

Hicket's smile turned to a chuckle. "Would you care for a rabbit or a fowl, milady?" he teased.

"I have sausages and carrots and onions. I would but need a fire."

"Sausages? And you stole nothing?" Robert asked.

"Only enough food for today. I would have eaten at Pynford today, so it is one day's food that I took."

"But you did no work at Pynford today."

"Robert!" Hicket spoke out. "She has worked far too hard for far too long. She is but a slip of a girl. Have some mercy." He smiled. "More, I would enjoy a good sausage."

So in a thicket by the ford of a stream they built a fire and Mila made the best dinner she had ever eaten in her entire life.

As they shared the food among them, the two friends relaxed and rested; they were tired, yet uneasy as they spoke of family and of a future now faded in the mist of uncertainty. And Mila listened, intent on not only their thoughts but on their language.

Years spent at a scullery sink, with little to occupy her quick mind and with the world of Pynford passing unseen at her back, had made Mila a listener. She knew the man who tended the garden because he spoke with different words than the monk who came by to beg bread. The bright haired girl who worked with herbs and spices, for all her haughty airs, spoke nothing like the ladies who spent their day in the mistress's chamber.

Robert and Hicket used words Mila did not always understand, and their voices were soft, like the mistress's ladies, muted by training in the young squires' schoolroom. In the time before she was strong enough to work in the kitchens, Mila had sometimes crept close enough to hear these lessons. It was the sound of the poetry they repeated that attracted her, and she, too, would repeat it often.

Sound and imagination had made her life at the scullery sink endurable. They also made Mila a mimic.

CHAPTER 10
Time for a Dangerous Scheme

Hicket had hoped for a longer respite, but the day was not yet gathering dusk.

Robert, who was anxious to reach Ricwyn before Balain's messenger found that Robert had left Pynford Castle and returned to Balian with that news, said, "It would seem impossible, but I believe if we travel at the same pace now, we can arrive at Ricwyn before dawn. I might have the chance to visit with my mother before Balian learns that I have left Pynford."

So they untethered the grazing horses from the grass near the stream, repacked their belongings and turned toward the darkening horizon, with Mila accepted as part of the group. She helped with the chores and mounted Luagor in the quietest manner, barely noticed by the preoccupied Robert—which was, for now, a good thing.

The road they traveled was a blur to her; she saw it, but again she did not. She had no memory of the path they followed or of the sky turning dark, but as they approached the village through the outlying fields, Ricwyn lay in darkness: few torches and lanterns burned in the paths that threaded through the cottages, outhouses and gardens. The cottages, too, were lightless and silent. Still, Robert hesitated to ride to the manse along those paths.

"We'll circle the hill and come through the trees at the back. That way we can be very near the house before we're actually on open ground. I know those wooded lands well. We can feel secure there."

The circle he chose through the wood was broad and he rode slowly, carefully, Hicket following closely at his back. Finally they entered a small clearing and Robert halted and swung down from his saddle. Hicket did the same and then turned to lift Mila to the ground.

"Wait here. Keep the horses still if you can. I'll go ahead." It was all Robert said. He left them there, disappearing into the trees with the silence of a specter.

Hicket was at a loss. Should he relieve the horses of their burden? What if Robert aroused the household and they had to leave quickly? But what if they were here for a long time? The horses needed to rest. How close was the manse? He didn't know. The darkness and the thickness of the surrounding wood made it almost impossible to see anything and no flicker of light invaded the space.

After standing still for a time, Mila grew anxious. "We should do something. The horses must need rest."

It made sense. Her face was just a pale oval at his

side, so he said nothing, but he moved to relieve Abatos of his heavy burden. That done he turned to the palfrey, removing Mila's bundle first. They had eaten the food and left the pot behind in an attempt to lighten the load of the horse that now carried two people, and still the bundle was heavy.

"What do you have here? Mila, have you taken something that belongs to Gregory?"

"No, no, nothing of the Lord Gregory's."

"But something, for certain. Nothing would not weigh so heavily in my hand." He took the cloak from the bundle and began to unravel it, first revealing the soft inner lining that shimmered softly even without light. "Mila, this cloak is of very fine cloth." He could not bring himself to say that it was not hers, but she felt his disbelief. Another moment and he was holding the wooden box, turning it, examining the finely carved surface. "Mila?"

Every surface was carved, so Hicket had no way to know which was the side that opened. "Is this a puzzle box?" He spoke almost to himself, still turning the heavy box from one side to another, feeling the carvings with his fingers. As he turned it one final time, the surface at the bottom fell away and the contents dropped to the ground, making a soft a thud in the thick layer of dead, decaying leaves. He stared down at it for time that could not be measured, then turned to her.

Two pale ovals faced each other across the darkness but neither spoke. At their feet rested a shining crystal globe encircled by two heavy golden chains that divided it into quadrants. The golden banded, blazing ball of light lit the small hollow it had carved into the leaves when it fell, lit it as if it had captured the light of the stars and held that light within itself.

"What is this? Where did you get this, Mila?" And then, convinced the answer would not be welcomed, "We must show this to Robert."

Far above Mila's head in the topmost branches of a towering tree an owl hooted.

CHAPTER 11
Mila Risks All to Help Robert

The night was still dark when Robert returned and found them asleep on the damp ground, horses tethered to a tree, belongings separated neatly in two piles ready to pack as quickly as possible should the need arise. Weary himself, he sat on the ground beside Hicket and shook him gently.

Hicket came awake quickly and sat up to face Robert. "What news?"

"None good, I fear. I wasn't able to reach my mother. Balian has guards posted by the gate, on both the inside and outside. This is something my father would do only in times of trouble."

"Is there no other way you might enter?"

"In normal times, yes. I was able to reach the top of the pale, but there are also unfamiliar men gathered within the yard. I was afraid to chance disturbing so many. And, again, my mother might be anywhere within. I feel certain that Balian has moved his wife and children into the family chamber. He would displace Emeline without regard as soon as possible."

Hicket sighed. The manse at Ricwyn was not familiar to him and he had no advice to offer.

Eager as she was to have Hicket distracted from the stolen crystal globe, Mila quickly offered a plan. "I might find your mother." They turned to look at the scraggly girl standing quietly beside the tree where Robert rested his back. He and Hicket were too amused to even consider what she said and, dismissing the thought, turned toward each other.

Mila knew better. "But I could find her. The servants in the kitchen would know where she takes her dinner. Think of it. I might be accepted in the kitchen. There is always a need for a scullery."

Robert swore. "God's bones."

Hicket reminded him that they were in the presence of a lady. Mila liked that, being called a lady, even if it was in jest.

Robert, though, ignored the reprimand. "God's bones," he repeated.

"Do you have a better plan?" she taunted him. She looked toward Hicket. "Do you?"

In truth, neither did. Hicket was ready to listen. "I could slip in with the daily workers as soon as it's light. I could go to the kitchen and ask to work for food."

Robert had little idea of the working of kitchens.

"Would they allow that? They must have what help they need. I believe that a stranger would not be welcome."

"I know only the kitchen at Pynford, but there it might be possible. It would depend on the tasks at hand and the number they have to do chores."

Hicket thought this over. "You say there are many new men quartered in the manse, Robert. Might the kitchen be hard put to provide for them?"

Mila was growing impatient. "If we are to try this, I must do it now. It will be light soon," she reminded them.

"And you are willing to do this?" Robert asked.

Willing to help Robert de Ricwyn? Mila could hardly believe her luck.

"Come then and I will take you to the main gate. It is the way the servants enter." Leaving Hicket with the horses, they set off through the wood together. Mila soon saw why Robert had warned Hicket and her to be silent; the pale of the manse was not that far off. Within a short distance, a circle of bare ground surrounded a knoll and the Ricwyn pale sat atop it.

In size and construction, it was no Pynford. She could not see the manse or any other buildings inside, but the wall atop the hillock was a simple wooden stockade set upon a pile of rough stone. As they circled to their left, the irregular tree line of the wood gave way to a symmetric orchard bordered on the village side by a small patch of land surrounded by a simple wattle fence. On the far side of the fenced area, the land sloped downward toward the open fields of the village, and the distance to the open path leading up to the manor stockade was far longer. At the front of the stockade where the gate was located, the path sloped directly toward the cottages of the village. This, then was the best route to take.

In the few minuets they had, Robert gave her a brief layout of the buildings she would find inside the pale: the manse; stables; kitchens and garden; chapel. It was too brief for her to form a visual image and confusing in front to back or side to side. But she had other concerns.

"Do many villagers come to the manse at daybreak?" she asked.

"I could not give you a good number. It was never of interest to me, and more, these seem to be different times."

"Will you wait for me here or return to Hicket?"

"You would get lost in the trees. I should wait here."

"Will you be safe here in daylight?"

"Safe nearby. I know the wood well." Then, looking down at the scruffy girl, he realized there was another concern. "If you do find my mother, she may not believe you came from me." He thought for a moment. "I fear that if I give you something of mine and you are discovered with it...." He considered this. "If you find her, tell her I never took the sword. Tell her I still refuse to accept the blame. She will understand."

As Mila turned to leave, he took her hand briefly. "You take a chance, Mila. Thank you." She turned away again so that he didn't see her smile.

As she approached the path to the village from the cover of the orchard she could see several men and women in rough clothing already gathered at the gate. The only person on the path toward the gate was a burly man carrying a heavy basket on his shoulders. He shuffled along slowly, weighed down by his load. Mila darted toward his back and was able to gain the path without him paying her heed. By the time he realized there was someone behind him, she had fallen in with his footsteps and he accepted that she had been there since he left the streets of the village.

By the looks of the crowd at the gate, the people were more than just villagers. Men made up a good part of the throng, men carrying tools and baskets of foodstuffs. When Mila and her supposed companion reached the gate, it was swinging open, the men guarding it not questioning many of the ragtag group entering from the path. They never gave Mila a second glance.

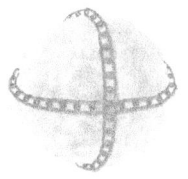

CHAPTER 12
Mila Dines with Rats

The yard of Ricwyn was not nearly the scale of the main yard at Pynford, and more, it seemed to be the only large space inside the manor ground. The stables strung along the wall to the east used much of this area as a stable yard. As Robert had described the space, Mila knew that the kitchen and its garden, and most likely other outer sheds like a buttery and henhouse, would be on the opposite side of the yard. She jostled through the crowd in that direction.

The main building rose along the back of the yard with stairs at the center leading to a great door. There was a smaller door at the bottom of the stair that led to a ground floor. At this time of the morning, both doors remained shuttered to the noise of the yard.

A low stone wall extended out from the manor building at the far side. The wall was no taller than she was and had only an open space at its center instead of a gate; but in other ways it bore likeness to the wall that separated the kitchens from the main yard at Pynford. Her way toward it was hampered by the unruly crowd of men in the yard, but she eventually pushed her way through the opening and found all she had hoped for: a garden squared off in the middle of some newer buildings that followed the same pattern of the kitchens at Pynford. They housed the buttery, the granary which was covered with oak shingles and, when she crossed to it and peered through the door, a good kitchen, its floor covered with stone. Within she saw a large fire and ovens—one large, the other smaller for the cakes—and two large tables at the center.

The scullery with its familiar stone sink was attached in a separate lean to. A boy not much above her own age was at work at the sink, pouring water from a bucket. She watched as he set the bucket down, took up his brushes and began scrubbing.

"Do you need more water?" He was startled and spun toward her. "I can fetch it for you."

"Who are you?" The front of his shirt was drenched to the waist, his dark hair hanging in clumps across his forehead.

"Mila. I was sent to help."

"Go then. Fetch more water." He returned to his task, and that was that. She took up the bucket and set off to find the well. There was none in the kitchen garden so she went back through to the main yard.

The only well at Ricwyn was near the center of this

space, a broad covered well with tall steps and a small trough. Mila found it impossible to lift the heavy bucket into the trough, but no one paid heed to her struggles; she was forced to dip water into the bucket one dipper at a time. When she returned to the scullery the boy was sitting on a stool beside the stone sink.

"Where were you?"

"The well is high. I had to dip the water."

He judged her stature through scowling eyes. "Aye. Fetching fresh water will be my task. But you can get the hot water from the cauldron in the kitchen. And you can help scrub." He handed her his brushes and poured rinse water from the bucket into the sink.

She was sweeping the last of the water into the drain when an old man shuffled in from the kitchen bearing a load of heavy pots. He set them in the sink and studied Mila, a stranger to him but not out of place in the scullery.

"Who are you, then?" he asked, but not in a way that seemed as if he were really interested.

"That's Mila," the dark haired boy said with authority. "She's here to help me."

The old man simply grunted, turned and left them.

The boy picked up the bucket. "Come, I'll show you where we get hot water."

They crossed the kitchen together; much like the one at Pynford, it was a steamy, bustling place where everyone concentrated on their own tasks. Most likely because she was with the boy, no one paid Mila any heed. He filled the scullery bucket with hot water from a cauldron set in one corner of the hearth and they returned to the scullery unnoticed.

Almost as if nothing in her life had changed, Mila's familiar routine began again.

The sun was well past its midday zenith when the work in the scullery slowed to a pace that allowed them to stop working for a time.

"We can eat now," the boy said, and she followed him to the kitchen.

A large pot was suspended over the fire, its contents bubbling in the heat. He swung it forward and dipped liberal portions of frumenty, a heavy pottage thickened with oats, into bowls he took from a shelf near the hearth and they went into the kitchen garden to eat.

The boy, Thomond they called him, was dark and spare and spoke with a different lilt than that Mila was most familiar hearing.

"Your voice is lovely," she began. Praise was as good as any means to avoid questions you don't want to answer. "You came here from another place."

"Aye, from across the sea."

"Across the sea?" Mila widened her eyes, impressed by the perils of such a journey.

"Aye." Thomond rarely enjoyed such an admiring audience. He nodded his head much as an elderly sage might. "A place of green fields and sparkling waters." He closed his eyes and Mila could feel his longing as the image of his home appeared before him. He sighed. "It was our own land once, but now there are new lords there, lords that come from this place. Butler men, not natives. My lord wanted to move his way up, but now it isn't easy for the natives to gain rank."

"Aye." Mila didn't understand all of this but felt it would be good to agree.

Thomond shrugged his narrow shoulders. "So he thought to join with the new group. Since they come from hereabouts, he crossed the sea to seek a new fealty in this land. Many of his men came with him. Me too."

Mila's imagination didn't extend to the reason a lord might bring someone like Thomond along on a sea journey, but that question would most likely cause the youth to prickle, so she left it be.

"How long have you been here?"

"In this land, two summers. But we only just came to Ricwyn. And soon we go back home, or near home. Across the sea again."

"That will be a dangerous journey," Mila said, as if increasing her admiration. "Thomond. It's an unusual name. Are many in your home across the sea called Thomond?"

"In truth, the land itself is called that way." He raised his chin as he said it.

Mila saw how that was. The boy was too insignificant to gain a name; he was in servitude or even a slave. He was part of an entourage that had come from a place across the sea, so in the kitchens he was known only by the name of that place.

She would like to learn more of that land, but for the present her interest must cleave close to Ricwyn. "The work today was heavy. Is it always this way?"

He seemed glad of the change of questions. "There are more and more men coming to Ricwyn every day. All must eat."

"And we are the worse for it." Mila set her empty bowl beside her, stretched and yawned, acting as if she were a comfortable part of the household.

"Aye," he agreed. Thomond had no problem with her. Mila was a boon to him, wherever she came from.

"Is the dinner over now? Has everyone had their meal?" It was important in the scullery where work only ended when cooking and eating ended.

"Most of it. We haven't had the end of the dinner in the great hall. The lord's retinue eats there. And then the bits from the family."

"Many?"

"Family, no. But the lord has many knights here now. I sense the number grows each day."

"Tell me about the family."

"The family? What would I know?"

"Only if there are many there, too. If we have much more work to do today." Mila wanted as much information as she could gather.

"Not much there. Some from the ladies, a bit from the

old Lady Emeline and her servant."

"She is not with the other ladies?"

"Her meal is sent on by itself, separate. The servant comes to fetch it."

"From the manor house?"

"Where else?" Thomond was growing annoyed.

Mila realized he was not a good source for what she had to know. She would press him no further. She leaned back to rest.

In time the old man from the kitchen came toward them. "More work for you two. Pots in the sink and I need someone to carry fresh trenchers to the hall."

Mila sprang up before Thomond could react. "I'll take them." She smiled toward Thomond and followed the man back into the kitchen where a large tray of fresh bread steamed on the central table. She lifted the heavy load awkwardly.

"Can you manage that?"

"I can," was all she said, and she was off.

She gave no thought to where she was going, but the hall would be easy enough to find.

She headed toward the opening that led to the main yard, but before she reached it a large man in a fairly clean pale tunic stopped her. He stood in a small doorway at the side of the manor house. "You there," he called. "Where are you taking that? This way."

She followed him down a few stone steps and through several stone arches of a great, low ceilinged storeroom under the manor. The floor was stone, too, uneven stone, and the place dark save for the few smoking lamps lit along the walls. She stumbled once almost dropping the heavy tray.

The man turned and warned, "Don't drop that." But he made no offer to help.

There were lanterns lit toward the center of the large, open cellar and soon they reached a flight of stone steps leading upward. The man climbed the first two. Mila was close behind him and thought she was meant to climb upward, too.

He stopped abruptly. "Not up there, fool." He took the tray from her. "The likes of you in the hall?" His brow furrowed and he turned away as he said, "Get back to the kitchen."

Mila, too, turned away, but back to the kitchen? Not likely. This vast, dim storage space filled with barrels and crates of all sizes, and better, located just under the great hall, seemed the better place to begin her search. She could well hide here, explore and eavesdrop.

But first things first.

She retreated along the way they had come, back through the stone archways along the uneven floor. When she stumbled earlier, a trencher had fallen off the tray. Thankfully the man from the hall didn't see it fall. Now it would be lovely to sit here, hidden from sight, and eat a bit of sweet smelling bread. Mila couldn't remember the last time she had warm bread. Maybe she never had.

Thankfully the rats had still not had time to attack the bread on the floor, though Mila was sure they were nearby. She could hear them scuffling. She scooped up the trencher and darted behind a pillar, stood still, listened; the only sounds were a muffled din from the great hall above and the occasional squeak from a scurrying rat.

Slowly, carefully, she retreated further into the dimness. Reaching the farthest wall, she crept along until she found a spot where dry goods were piled almost to the arched stone ceiling. Surrounded by casks and storage chests, she settled onto the damp floor to scoff her unexpected treasure.

She ate quickly, but then what to do next? Dinner in the hall was still going on; occasional shouts and cheers echoed from above. Once someone trudged down the stair and she could hear them fill pitchers from a cask closer to the center of the room, though Mila couldn't see if it was the same man who took the trenchers from her. Tired from a full day in the scullery and full to bursting for the second time in as many days, she savored this moment of rest. She leaned her back against a large wooden crate and, before she realized it, was fast asleep.

CHAPTER 13
Prowling the Cellars of Ricwyn Manor

A large thud somewhere nearby awakened Mila with a start. Suddenly alert, her first instinct was to huddle further into a corner of her retreat, becoming a small dark spot in a small dark hole. A second thud made her flinch. "Is that the last of it, then?" It was a man's voice, rough and low.

"One more," another man answered and Mila heard them retreat toward the main passageway.

She didn't move. She barely breathed. Waiting. Waiting.

One more. So they were coming back. This time she heard them, heard the creaking of a door in the front wall and thought it must be the door under the great stairs in the main yard. Heavy footfalls tromped down a few stone stairs and feet shuffled along uneven stones. They turned into the same archway Mila had chosen and came toward the back wall following her path, but their progress was slow, labored. Then another thud.

"Was a heavy one."

"Aye," came the reply. "Heavy. What is our Balian storing up now?"

"More weapons? Armor? I'd not be surprised at that. He has plans, has this lord."

"I hope the likes of us are not to be part of it."

The only reply to that was another grunt. If they were serfs of the manor house or even lower down the labor scale, Mila knew they would have no choice in that. She listened to the retreating footsteps, the creaking door, then nothing. Aside from some scraping rats, only silence.

Silence.

Something was missing.

She began to move, first lifting her head then slowly shifting to the front of her hidden hole. Rising up, she peered out into the dim, silent space. Listening.

Where was the murmur from the hall above her, the shouts or cheers, the rumble of voices, the music played in the background? Those sounds no longer seeped into the cellar. The room above was quiet now. She squeezed her eyes tight and shook her head. How long had she slept, content and comfortable in the good fortune of fresh, warm bread? She had no way of knowing if it was early evening or late night. Would she be granted the cover provided by a long sleeping household, or was it near to dawn?

She had no choice. Robert depended on her, was even now waiting for her. She crept forward toward the arch along the main passage. The heavy trunks the men had dropped stood close to this arch, but there was a second path along the inside of the arches, too, a smaller passage, albeit cluttered with goods that would slow her advance in this dim light. Still, it would be the safer route. If someone came down the stair from the hall or in through the door from the kitchens, they would see her if she were in the main passageway. On this inner side of the arches she would be hidden from view.

Using this route, slowly, carefully, making less noise than even the scuffling rats, Mila made her way around boxes and barrels toward the foot of the main stair.

It was an opened stairway, this entrance to the upper hall, steps of a kind she had never seen before. At Pynford the inner stairs were built within the thickness of the walls. Here though, a stone balustrade lined both sides of the steps, but the balustrade was no higher than her waist. Aside from supporting pillars at every third or fourth step, Mila could see above the staircase and through into the far side of the lower floor. This other side seemed different from the one she crept through. When she got nearer she realized that it was quite different: not storage but sleeping quarters. In that space, more lamps lit the back wall, and pegs between them were hung with shirts and tunics. Knights or more likely squires or even house servants of higher rank must sleep here. Short of creeping into the space, Mila had no way of knowing which. Her only concern was that whoever was there was well asleep.

It was brighter near the bottom of the stair, too. Lanterns were suspended on the pillars at either side of the stair and they burned with smoky light. Now, with more light shed on them, Mila's curiosity couldn't escape the containers filling the passage. Straw poked through the sides and tops of many and seemed to fill those that had no tops; packing straw meant that the contents needed protection for transport and storage; the need for protection meant that they contained something of value. Even in her precarious circumstances, Mila couldn't resist something of value.

She poked a hand into the top layer of straw of the nearest opened box. Something hard, cold, rounded, but with spikes and, further around, a chain. A mace. Surely weapons. No wonder the boxes were heavy. She poked further into the straw. There was another mace in the box, and, a little further down, a hilt, a rather small hilt with a ring at the end. Slowly, her deft hand clutched it and pulled it from the straw.

It was a small dagger, certainly not bigger than a kitchen knife. Perhaps just the size of a table knife. But it was never that. The blade was wide at the center, narrow at both ends and curved in an arc, the point skewed at an angle away from the hilt, and it was sharpened to a dangerous edge.

She held the knife up toward the smoky light; it truly was unlike anything she had ever seen. The metal ring at the end of the hilt was brighter than the hair of the golden haired girl; it gleamed in the flickering light.

Without warning, the door across from the bottom of the stair creaked as it was pulled outward. Startled, Mila darted behind the box and slipped back into the shadows.

Two boys not more than her own age came in and trudged down the few stone steps to the stone floor. They were a disgruntled pair, complaining much like the men she had heard earlier.

"How many horses can he stable?" one asked, though it wasn't a question as much as a gripe.

"Shouldn't all be left to us!"

Squires, she thought, or close to it. Stable boys would sleep with the horses, but these two made their way to the far side of the stair and down the arched passage on that side. She listened to them go then slid down the back wall to wait once again.

Silence. From here she could hear some snores or snorts, some shifting, but it was the silence of a house at rest. After what seemed a safe time, Mila crept forward to the bottom of the stair. The knife was still in her hand, so she slipped it under her belt. Waited again.

Well, if she hoped to help Robert....

CHAPTER 14
The Lady Emeline

The stair was wide across, but the steps were steep and narrow. She crept up them slowly, hugging one side and stopping to listen often. It was dark toward the top, darker than below. Mila had to let her eyes adjust. At the head of the staircase, she crouched next to a pillar, listened again. Only the sounds of a household asleep.

She peered out into the dimness. The only light came from fires burning at each end of one large room that was divided by the stairs. The part of the room toward the kitchen garden was smaller, the fire at its end closer to the stair. In that space, a large bed was set on the floor before a stone chimney. There was a wardrobe next to the bed and a door next to that. From the nearness of the fire and the door in the wall, Mila guessed that there was another chamber on that side of the manor, a private place beyond the great hall for the lord and his family. Robert had mentioned such a chamber; it was not a place she would want to explore.

On the other side of the separating stair was a larger space. She could make out several large trestle tables and benches along the back wall and then an empty area closer to the fire. She turned into that room and crept forward to the nearest table. It was broad and she was able to slip under it and crawl toward the fire.

The open area near the fire was covered with bodies. Men—many men. They were sleeping on mats packed so close to each other that she knew she would never be able to move among them.

Still, to what purpose? Surely Lady Emeline would not be here.

Mila crawled back to the other end of the table and slipped to the top of the stair again. She studied the wall facing her, the back wall of the manor house. Robert said there was a small chapel attached to the back of the manor, "A proper chapel," he called it, "covered with tiles, with a portable altar and a wooden cross." She remembered his words—remembered that he seemed more proud of the chapel than he was of the manor itself. The entrance to that chapel must be somewhere along this back wall. She searched the dark stones for an opening, but in the gloom it was impossible to see. It would be good to find it.

Again she crept from the top of the stairs, this time crossing to the back wall. Right toward the lord's chamber or left toward the sleeping men? She held her breath and began moving right.

When she was halfway to the bed before the fire, she backed away from the wall and surveyed its rough stone surface carefully. Heavy tapestries covered the wall from this point to the corner, but none reached the floor as the covering of a doorway would. So it was not here.

She moved close to the wall again, into the shadowy place at the meeting of the wall and floor, and turned to her left. She passed the head of the staircase and was almost at the corner of the hall when she found it: an opening draped with heavy cloth.

A sleeper in the hall coughed loudly spawning a ripple of shifts along the mats. Mila held her breath. Best act quickly. She lifted a corner of the cloth and saw that whatever space lay beyond was in complete darkness. She slipped through the opening and slid down to the floor, resting her back against the wall. Once again her eyes adjusted to another level of light as she tried to determine just where she was.

She soon realized that the blackness wasn't total. Two slits of pale gray night sky showed through windows set high in a wall at the far end of what was a small room. The air was fresher here, too, and colder. And there was little sound, with noises seeping in from the hall muffled by the heavy drape.

A small empty room. Nothing.

Best to leave this seeming dead end before night gave way to morning and she was exposed. She bent forward, planning to crawl through the curtain and return the way she had come, but as her eyes swept the floor she saw it: a sliver of light from under a door. So there was another entrance to this space.

She changed direction, crawled toward the light. Not a door, but another curtain of sorts. She reached out and touched it. Heavy, much like the one she had come through. Again she lifted a corner and peered through.

This room had no great fire but was lit by lamps. Mila could see one high on the far wall. There was something else alight, too, along the wall near this entry. It cast more light than the lamp she could see, penetrating the room with flickering shadow.

Mila had to poke her head into the room and peer over her shoulder to see what it was, a fatal mistake. An old woman sat next to a burning brazier set on a stone table. Clearly she had seen the curtain move and now stared directly into Mila's eyes. Both were startled, shocked into stillness. Neither moved.

At last the woman spoke in a mere whisper, and it was with a kindness Mila had no reason to expect. "Come in, child. You are frightened. Do you know where you are?"

Mila crawled through the curtain and stood before the woman. "I thought this was the chapel."

"You have never been to the chapel?"

"Never."

"So you are new to Ricwyn?" Even the sculleries were welcomed in the chapel.

"I came today."

"And so you seek the chapel?" By the deep folds in her dark cloak, Mila realized that the woman was richly dressed in soft wool. She was gentle, too: she seemed almost concerned about a tattered chit obviously from the ranks of lower servants.

This might be a good time to cry. Mila blinked several times, not difficult given the sudden brighter light. Finally a tear slid down one cheek.

"Come nearer."

Mila took a step toward the table.

"We must be quiet." The woman pointed to a maidservant asleep on a straw mat in front of a raised bed in the far corner of the room. "What brings you in search of the chapel at this early hour?"

So it was early, probably nearer morning. Mila's eyes swept the walls. There was an opening in one—a tapestry covering what must be a low door. She was judging its size even now as she stepped closer to the woman. She guessed that she might slip out that way.

"Child? What brings you in search of the chapel?"

"I do not know this place, my lady. In truth I was sent to find..."

"To find?"

She had to hope; she had to try. "To find the Lady Emeline."

"You seek the Lady Emeline? But for what reason?"

Mila hung her head, blinked again, forcing more tears.

"For what reason, child?"

"Her son, My Lady. He wishes to speak with her."

The old woman shifted on the stool where she sat, glanced again at the sleeping maid servant and then into the fire burning in the brazier. After a little time she looked into Mila's eyes. It was a steady, penetrating gaze.

"Which son, child?"

"Robert, My Lady."

The old woman let out a deep sigh. It was as if she had been holding her breath since Mila first mentioned a son of Ricwyn and now something she had come to dread had happened. As if now she knew the worst.

But her gaze held steady. Whatever it was that she feared, she was a woman of strength; she would not turn away from it.

"You were sent to me by Robert?"

"You My Lady?"

"I am Robert's mother."

Mila studied her closely in the flickering light. She was a tall woman; even seated, she was almost as tall as Mila was standing. Her face was lined with age, but it was a noble face, and the strong line of the nose was familiar. She could be the Lady Emeline; then again, she might not be.

"You doubt me."

"It is of grave importance to Robert."

"And you must be certain." She rose and crossed to a chest, lifted the lid carefully and withdrew a box. She left the chest lid opened, as if afraid any noise would wake her servant, and brought the box back to the table. "Can you read child?" Stupid question. "No." She smiled at her own idea. "Still, these are messages from my children. I would that you could read them as you would see most are from Robert.

"I can see that you must be his mother. I see him in you."

This made the old woman smile. "But how might I be assured that you come from Robert?"

"A sword, My Lady. Robert said he never took the sword and even now refuses to take the blame."

Emeline, for it must be Emeline, smiled at that, too. "No, I never truly believed he did. Balian was responsible, most likely; it could never be proved." Now she studied the wretched girl who stood before her with such ease. "Robert did well to trust you, child. Did you come all the way from Pynford Castle?"

"With Robert, My Lady. He is here. He wishes to see you."

"Robert is here?"

"Not within the manor. He waits nearby."

Emeline sighed again, seemingly relieved at the news that Robert was not in the manor. "Yes, and I must speak with him." The maidservant stirred and Emeline looked toward her. "Robert was wise to not come inside Ricwyn manor himself. But is there another place we can meet?"

"He hoped you might come to him."

"Nearby, you say?"

"The orchard, My Lady. Might you come to the

orchard?"

"It may be possible. Yes. Today, if the weather is fair, I might visit the orchard with no one objecting."

"I will take the message to him, My Lady."

"But how will you leave the manor without being seen?"

Mila smiled. "I will. No one really looks at me, My Lady." Emeline seemed saddened by this. "That is a door, My Lady?"

"This is the room the priests use. They come and go by that small door."

"Where is it within the pale of the manse?"

CHAPTER 15
Lost in the Wood

Leaving Ricwyn unnoticed proved far easier than Lady Emeline or even Mila believed it would have been. Robert's mother was living in a small room to the side of the Ricwyn chapel, a chamber still used by clergy. Because the land sloped upward slightly from the front to the back of the manor, the door in this chamber was not as high as the main door to the hall at the front and just a few steps from the ground. Though she was unfamiliar with the route, Mila preferred it to retracing her steps through the hall, down the stair and through the cellar.

Lady Emeline, though, feared for Mila's safety while passing through the yard and out the main gate.

"It is best if I leave early in the morning when the peasants from the village come to work in the manor," Mila explained. "The men at the gate will not take notice of another such."

Lady Emeline saw how it was, but she also feared for

Mila alone in the yard in the darkness. "It will be light soon. It might be best if you wait here until almost dawn and then slip out and cross to the gate where you can wait near the stable wall. Here, see this." She tore a small corner of vellum from one of the letters she had taken from the box and scratched a rough outline of the yard and stables. "There are many new men here with horses and servants. So many that you may be taken for one of the new servants." She smiled. "Unnoticed." Unnoticed suddenly seemed a good thing to the old woman. "Now we must be quiet and await the best hour for you to go."

As Mila studied the drawing in the light from the brazier, Lady Emeline glanced again at her sleeping servant. "Remember, child, you must trust no one. Now it will be better if this room is dark. I will return to my bed." She took the soft shawl from her shoulders and wrapped it around Mila. "It will keep you warm as you wait, but you must leave it here with me."

Mila smiled in return. They both understood that a shawl of that value would be noticed. She crossed to the door as the old woman dampened the fire and moved to her bed, silently easing over the woman on the mat.

Mila stood behind the tapestry and pushed the small door outward a crack, watching for the first sign of the lightening of dawn. As she waited an owl somewhere outside in the yard hooted softly, not once but several times. It was an oddly comforting sound to her now. Not a warning of danger, though danger surely lurked; more a sign that she was not alone.

Standing here at the door, waiting in silence, her thoughts strayed to Robert and Hicket and even to Lady Emeline, whose words wrapped her in a comfort warmer even than the soft shawl: "Robert did well to trust you, child." No, she was no longer alone.

When the first light colored the sky, Mila slipped the soft shawl from her shoulders and left the manor. As she turned the corner into the main yard, men were already about, most drifting toward the well; a young boy was hauling buckets of water toward the stables and another filling a trough under the stable overhang. She could hear whinnies within the long building as she passed, but no one stopped to question her.

She hesitated, was about to slip into the niche Emeline had described in her drawing, a small space between the end of the stable and the stone base of the wooden stockade that surrounded the manor yard, when someone called out to her.

"Mila!"

She turned to see Thomond coming toward her from the well. "Mila, is that you then?" He quickened his pace; clearly he was not pleased.

At that moment the guards swung the gate wide to admit the workers from the village. Peasants in drab tunics very much like her own streamed between them and she was able to escape into their midst. A large man with a crooked staff herded a goat and two fat squealing pigs through the opening; he had a small child with him, a scruffy mischief-maker who ran here and there as if to help herd the animals but only added to the chaos. Mila was able to dart behind them and then out onto the path. Free of the manor yard but still not free of the danger of Thomond following her, calling out, sending the guard at the gate after her, she hurried down the slope as quickly as she could without arousing further attention and turned toward the orchard.

"Robert is waiting for me," she said over and over to herself. "Robert will be there." She was well within the orchard, trees growing in ordered rows surrounding her, when she began to doubt.

She ran now, through the orchard and into the denser trees that marked the beginning of the demesne. This was the lord's land, preserved for his use only; a peasant with no license had no right to be here. Still the fear of Thomond raising the hue and cry for a servant who had no right to leave the manse led her to keep running.

Robert knew this wood well, but Mila, stumbling through the undergrowth with a canopy of trees shutting out the faint light of dawn, was lost within a short time. At last aware of her surroundings, of the danger they posed, she stopped. Listened. Nothing. She was alone. Alone on the demesne of an unknown master.

She should go back toward the orchard, wait at the edge of the wood for Robert to come to her. "He will come," she said again, this time repeating it out loud, as if to convince herself. She turned round determined to return to the orchard, but the ordered rows of trees had disappeared.

She turned round and round, searching for a path. How long had she run? And from which direction? Once again, she was alone.

And then he was there. She continued to turn slowly, to search the surrounding wood, and suddenly he was there, right beside her.

"Mila?"

Unaware of the tears streaming down her cheeks, Mila closed her eyes, opened them again, looked up at him. A sudden streak of morning sunlight filtered through the canopy of trees blurring his face with shadow, and his smile was hidden to her.

"Mila, you are afraid." His arms grasped her and he swept her up off the ground. "I'm here child. You are safe with me."

CHAPTER 16
A Knife that Cuts Both Ways

Mila followed him as they made their way through the undergrowth quietly, with Robert holding low branches aside for her and lifting her over fallen logs. He stopped to listen often, assuring himself that they were alone in the forest. She had not run as far into the wood as she first thought she had, and Hicket and the horses were closer than she expected.

They found Hicket resting with his back to a tree trunk, his eyes closed and his face drawn, but he sprang up as soon as he heard them enter the small clearing.

"Are you tired, my friend?" Robert asked. "It has been a hard two days for us."

"A bit weary, Robert, but gaining strength every day. Tell me, what news?"

Robert turned to her. "Yes, Mila, what news? Were you able to discover if my Lady Mother stays within Ricwyn?"

"More, Robert. I spoke with her."

"Spoke with her?" His concern was foremost, rising to the surface before his curiosity. "She is well?"

"I believe so. I did not know her before, but I saw nothing to make me believe otherwise. She seemed well."

"Where is she?"

"In a chamber next to the chapel. It is a small room with no fire, but she had a brazier burning and the space is comfortable."

"She was alone?" Robert seemed troubled to think she might be.

"There was a maidservant with her, but she was asleep by Lady Emeline's bed."

"So Balian has seen fit to give her a bed and a servant and a chamber. Rosalind will not be pleased with that."

"From what you have told me of Balian, Robert, Rosalind will have no say," Hicket said. Through their years as comrades and friends, he had learned more of Robert's family than Mila knew.

"Rosalind?" she asked.

"Balian's good wife." Robert's answer was sarcastic. "Every bit as proud as Balian and," he paused "—yes, as greedy—though I flinch from the thought. She would begrudge a servant air if she thought it might diminish her own."

Mila was surprised at his vehemence. "She would not want the Lady Emeline living with her in the family chamber?"

"Rosalind would not want the beautiful and well

beloved Emeline living at all, if she could find a way to arrange that."

Robert's vicious tone revealed even more than the cruel sentiment, and both the tone and sentiment shocked Hicket. "Robert, this is not like you. Surely you go too far."

"I wish it were so." Robert frowned, but remained unmoved. "Believe me, Hicket, Rosalind envies Emeline, begrudges her grace, begrudges the admiration my mother has earned from those above and below her status. It is true. Now that Rosalind is finally mistress of Ricwyn, she will often be compared to the last mistress and found wanting." He clenched his fists as these thoughts only raised more concern.

In an attempt to ease Robert's mind, or at least distract his thoughts, Hicket turned to Mila. "Tell us how you were able to enter Ricwyn without being stopped."

At the question, Robert's thoughts returned to the present and he added, "And tell us what you discovered, Mila."

She told them how she slipped through the gate unnoticed, and then through the yard with the many men there; she spoke of the overworked kitchens and scullery and of Thomond who came from across the sea with others who traveled from the same land. She told of the storage space filled with arms, of the stables burdened with too many horses, and of the large number of knights who slept in the hall. At last she told Robert of Emeline living in the chamber next to the chapel, of her kindness.

Both Robert and Hicket were amazed at the cunning of this slip of a girl.

"Lady Emeline promises to come to the orchard today, if she is able," Mila told them.

"If she is able?" Robert's concern deepened. "Is she not free to do as she wishes?"

"That I cannot say. I know only that she was anxious not to wake the maidservant who is with her, and that she told me to trust no one."

Robert frowned again, his lips drawn together against his teeth.

Hicket put his hand on Robert's shoulder. "Have no fear for your mother, Robert. She will come."

Robert had no answer to this, so after a moment Hicket again turned to Mila. "Now, thief," he said lightly, "is that something I see tucked under your belt? What did you manage to bring us from the kitchen?"

"Alas, Sire," Mila bowed and mimicked his tone, as she withdrew the small knife, "it is not food, but only this dagger."

Robert looked at the beautiful object with the oddly curved blade, then from one to the other of his companions. He rolled his eyes upward.

Hicket took the knife from her and studied it, turning it slowly in his hand. "A karambit," he said.

"You know this weapon?" Robert asked.

"I have seen one before. A carpenter in my village used one for many years. It is more than just a weapon, Robert.

The karambit has many functions. Aye, it could be a weapon of self-defense in times of need, but this blade and ring offer advantages over other types of knives. The curve provides extra reach and allows the knife to be used upside-down."

Robert was fascinated, his thoughts now absorbed by the practical shape of a knife blade.

"And the ring?" Mila wanted to know.

"The ring offers a secure grip. It allowed the carpenter precision and stability when he was working at odd angles." Hicket put his forefinger through the ring and held the knife as if he were going to use it to strike out. He swiped at the air with the odd blade and then, simply by flicking his wrist, swiped in the opposite direction. "See, if it is used as a weapon, you can strike in many directions and are able to hold it in a way that makes it almost impossible to have it pulled from your grip. And more, because of the ring it will not slip backward in your hand. In a weapon, this is important, especially if you are not strong." He smiled down at Mila. "But think of it, too, as a tool. The ring provides a grip that proves useful when the conditions are, say, slippery, as they might be in a kitchen, or if it is wet or icy." He handed the knife back to her.

She examined it, felt its weight in her hand.

"You should begin to use it, Mila," Hicket advised. "Feel comfortable with it in your hand. It will serve you well."

Mila grasped it as Hicket had and swiped at the air,

flicking her wrist in one direction and another.

Hicket smiled at her first clumsy attempts. "We must practice."

She swiped at the air again and Robert thought, "Just what we need, a thief with a knife."

CHAPTER 17
Emeline Comes into the Forest

Dawn turned into a bright summer sky. As the sun rose higher, Robert left Mila and Hicket with the horses and found cover in the forest near the edge of the orchard where he waited for his mother to come to him. He was prepared to wait for many hours, but Emeline, as anxious to see her son as he was to see her, came while it was still early morning.

She and her servant walked down the path from the manor and toward the orchard wearing broad brimmed straw hats, each with an empty sack swinging from her belt. They skirted the trees at the perimeter of the orchard and made their way to the fenced area where together they pulled open a heavy gate and disappeared within.

"Strawberries," Robert thought. "There will still be some ripening."

After what seemed to Robert a long time Emeline came out of the gate alone, and turned into the orchard. As she approached the edge of the wood, Robert moved nearer and called to her.

Emeline lifted her eyes and searched the trees, eager to find him. "Robert?"

"Here, Mother. Just come forward."

When she saw him her face lighted with a broad smile and she ran to join him, stumbling through the undergrowth in her haste. He caught her up in his arms and realized she was trembling.

"Oh, Robert. I didn't think you would want to return to Ricwyn."

He held her for a moment and then, signaling her to silence, pulled her farther into the wood. "I am not certain I should return, Mother. Before I make that choice, I would best know what Balian has in mind for me."

"What Balian has in mind for any of us, Robert. That is the question."

"But you are well? He treats you well?"

"Well enough. There are many changes and it is happening very fast, as if it were planned for quite some time."

"We must talk, then. Not here. Come with me."

But Emeline was reluctant. She glanced over her shoulder, back at the opened gate of the strawberry garden. "Rosalind has given me a new servant, Robert. One I do not know well and do not trust."

"Just for a short time then," he insisted. "We will devise a story to account for a short absence."

Emeline trusted this son above all her other children, trusted him enough to follow him through the dense forest to the small clearing where Hicket and Mila waited.

Emeline saw Mila first, and again her face lighted with the broad smile that had always made her the most beloved of mistresses. "Ah, child, you are safe."

Mila smiled, too, but was too overcome by Emeline's sincere concern to speak.

Robert still grasped his mother's hand, as if she were in danger of disappearing. "So you know Mila," he said, amazed at his mother's ready acceptance of the scrubby child. "And this is my friend Hicket."

Hicket bowed to the great lady who through the years was at the center of many of Robert's stories; but he shifted his head as he did, not wanting to confront her with the horror of his scarred face and blind eye. It was an act of self-consciousness from someone who did not really know Emeline.

She took both his hands and drew him toward her, looking up at him and again smiling, though this smile was wistful. "You are friend enough to be willing to come to Ricwyn with Robert," she turned to include Mila in this sentiment, "to come with him not knowing what you would find here. You must love my son very much."

Mila, resourceful as she was, did not know how to accept these words from Emeline. Her head fell forward and she stared at the ground.

At Emeline's words, Robert, too, was suddenly aware

of the loyalty that he had long come to expect from Hicket. In truth, he hoped it was loyalty in both directions, something they could both take for granted. The thought of loyalty from Mila, though, was unfamiliar, unexpected. The child stood before them, her head down so that he could not see her face.

A child? Perhaps not quite.

Shifting his thoughts toward his mother, he broke the spell she had cast. "Time passes, Mother. What is the news? You are no longer living with the family?"

Emeline was quick to join the present and answer him. "Rosalind insisted that the family chamber was now hers alone, though she had lived there with us these many years. I had hoped to join a convent, but Balian refused to have me move from the manse. I am not certain of his reasons, Robert. Nonetheless, the priest's room next to the chapel suits me very well."

"But you have a maidservant who you feel is set to spy on your movements. This cannot be comfortable. Why is it that Balian would want you watched?"

"Your brother fears I know too much of what he plans, and he does not want his plans known to others."

"And do you?"

"Do I know his full plans? In truth, I believe I know little. Still, what I do know may be of value to others. I see messengers come and go from the manor, sometimes in the dark of night. Balian has gathered many new men here, too, knights and also rough men who are preparing for combat." Her eyes narrowed in thought and she grew even more anxious as she looked up at her favorite son. "Balian must have laid his plans quietly over time, for the men appeared in groups and in a matter of days. It began to happen soon after you left, even before Edmund...." Her voice trailed off, as if she were unable to speak of the death of her husband.

"He has gathered stores of weapons, too," Robert told her. "Mila saw these."

Emeline turned to study Mila, though not in a severe manner. It was more as if to gauge the wit, the ability, of this scullery; it was surely above what her appearance would lead one to guess. At last Mila looked up at her and they both smiled.

Emeline continued, "I know from Roland that Balian has plans to send him on a mission to Ireland. He spoke of the river Usk and a town on the place where the river inters the sea, a town called Caerleon that is frequented by mariners."

"Thomond came to Ricwyn with men from Ireland," Mila said. Emeline knew nothing of Thomond or the men who brought him, so Mila was forced to explain, which she did in a halting manner. For all her grace and sincerity, the status of Lady Emeline still made Mila hesitant.

"Yes, the message Balian sent to Pynford was that Roland was to go to Ireland," Robert told her.

"So it must be that the men gathered at Ricwyn are to go to Ireland with Roland, though this seems wrong.

Surely Roland should not be chosen to lead a fighting force." Emeline knew her children well.

"I would be a better choice in this?" Robert asked her.

"You would be the obvious choice, Robert. Roland will be..." She searched for a word.

"A steward in armor. I do not say that unkindly, Mother. Roland has a talent for organization that most lack. And more, he is a good and honest man. But he is not made for a mission such as I fear Balian plans." He hesitated, then asked, "Would you prefer that I go in his place?"

Emeline started at this. "No! No, Robert. You must not become involved in any plans that Balian has made. We both know of Balian's ambition. It will lead to no good."

"Balian is unscrupulous," Robert told her. "He sent to Gregory of Pynford asking for me to return to Ricwyn. Did you know that?"

"No." It was news, but not surprising news. "But of course!" She nodded. "Ah, now his actions make sense. His plan was never to send Roland alone. Roland is to be sent only to accompany you."

"And Balian sends us forth with a fighting force." Robert's brow furrowed. "What is he hoping to achieve?" He considered this. "Land will be the first priority, an expansion of the Ricwyn holdings. But perhaps good will is his primary goal."

"Good will?" Hicket asked.

It was Emeline, schooled over many years in family diplomacy and aware of the manner of feudal expansion, who answered him. "We know that there has been unrest in these lands across the sea for many years, invasions from here that were supported by both the crown and the church. If Balian knows that there are more powerful forces seeking lordship over territory in Ireland, then he may believe he would gain greatly by assisting them." She gave this more consideration. "Yes, I believe that Balian would wish to take part in this invasion."

Robert clenched his fists and began pacing. "But why the secrecy, if all this is generally known? Certainly Balian would not undertake such an effort without the consent and even the assistance of higher lords?" He stopped abruptly and addressed his mother. "He would not even consider doing this on his own!" They looked at each other in a way that made Hicket understand that both believed Balian would. "If what we believe is indeed true, Gregory of Pynford is one who should be informed of it."

Emeline agreed. "Yes, Gregory and the many other lords Ricwyn owes allegiance."

"And we both fear that these plans have not been shared with them?"

"It is the most reasonable explanation, Robert. Why else would Balian attempt to keep it secret from me? He even keeps Roland away from me."

"And from me," Robert added. "No, this force that he assembles is a secret force." Again his fists clenched. "He sends it without the knowledge or consent of those he owes allegiance."

The tightly knit bond of feudal fealties was something even Mila could understand, and she was aware of the tension growing in Robert. He turned his back on them, stared into the trees, shoulders square, hands clenched.

Emeline stared down at the ground, quietly waiting for her young son to gather his thoughts. She saw it then, not in the undergrowth where Mila had kicked it aside in her eagerness to have it forgotten, but closer, just at the root of a large tree.

"What is this?" She took a step toward the object in the grass, a globe of crystal that suddenly seemed to send forth more light. She reached down and lifted it with both hands, stared into its depths, then sent a questioning glance from Hicket to Mila and back.

"It belongs to Mila," Hicket explained.

Emeline looked down at the girl. "But it cannot. How did you come by it, Mila?"

Mila reddened, turned away, so Emeline again looked toward Hicket.

"It was with her when we found her leaving Pynford," he explained.

"Was it at Pynford, then?" Emeline asked her. "Mila, tell me. Did you find this at Pynford?"

Mila refused to turn and face them.

"Mila?" Hicket reached out and touched her shoulder.

Now Robert, too, became interested.

"I found it in the cloak of a traveler who slept in the great hall. I never meant to take it." The words tumbled out in a rush. "It was in my way. I tried to move it, but once I lifted the box, I knew that it was too heavy to set down."

"Too heavy to set down?" Robert was puzzled.

At last she turned and looked up at him. "The box was heavy and hard. I could not see the floor well in the dark, and so I feared that if I tried to set it down again, it would make a sound."

"But why should a sound be a problem?"

Hicket took over. "It was dark in the hall, Mila? You were there, in the hall of Pynford Castle, in the dark of night." He nodded at the certainty of this idea. "You were there to steal something?"

"I only wanted a cloak. A warm cloak. I had nothing."

"So you went to the hall in the night to steal a cloak and came away with this crystal, too?" Robert was growing angrier.

"Robert," Emeline interrupted to calm him, "it is more. This is not a mere object one could steal. It is the Orb of Hurstmontfort."

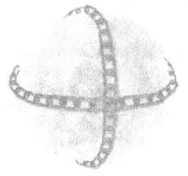

CHAPTER 18
The Mystery of the Orb

They stood by silently as Robert took the crystal from his mother and turned it slowly in his hands, gazing into its depths, mesmerized. Hicket, too, was captured by its beauty, and both young men realized that this orb must have immense value.

A sphere the size of Robert's massive fist, it was pure crystal of a kind that seemed to glow from within. The surface was cut into a regular pattern of crossing lines and sparkled even in the dimness of the forest. A heavy golden chain surrounded the crystal along a center axis and in two directions, dividing the globe into four equal quadrants. It was a treasure beyond anything they had seen before.

Robert shook his head slowly, though not moving his gaze from the crystal. "I've never seen the like. The Orb of Hurstmontfort, Mother?" he asked.

"Hurstmontfort is a village to the east, nearer the town

of Lincoln," Emeline began. "I have heard many bards tell this tale. According to legend, the orb belonged to the village, but no one knows how the orb first came to be there, only that it had rested in a secret place in the church of Hurstmontfort for as far back as the villagers could remember.

"But then, again in a time in the far distant past, the orb disappeared from the church. It is an object of great value, so people believed it had been stolen by someone from the village or even by a band of thieves. All that is certain is that the orb was gone."

"Until?" Hicket asked.

"Until not so many summers past. And the tale surrounding its return holds even more mystery. It made people believe that the orb has powers."

Robert was skeptical. "Magic." He scowled at the thought, knowing it would not be something he could believe.

Emeline, though, had a differing opinion. "No, I have not heard it told as magic. The tale holds that the orb was returned to the village by a younger son of the Montfort family. He found it in a nearby wood at the root of a sweet chestnut tree. But it was not well concealed. The thought was that, had the orb rested for all those many years in the place where the boy found it, then it would have been discovered long before. It led the villagers to believe that the orb itself decided when it should return, that there was a reason for its reappearance at that exact time."

"The reason being?" Robert asked. Mila was relieved to see that he was at least more interested in the orb than the thief now.

"The tale is not straightforward." She took the orb from Robert and held it out so that they all could see it as she continued her story.

"It seems the villagers soon thought to send the orb to York. Some say it was the Montfort family that decided this. It is a valuable object and the family has roots there, so perhaps they wanted to keep it safe. Or perhaps they only wanted to possess it. Still others say that the orb, upon its return, brought destruction and death to the village, so that the villagers wished to be rid of it.

"Whatever the reason for the removal of the orb, during the journey of the pilgrims to carry the orb to York many different forces sought to steal it, including even the church in the person of the bishop of Lincoln." She paused. "And this is where the legend gained greater strength; for once again the orb came to be thought of as an object that chooses its own path. Each time an attempt was made to take it away from the villagers, the orb could not be removed. Over and over, it returned to the same person. Just as it seemed to reappear in the village in its own good time, so it is believed that the orb continued to choose those who would possess it."

"And the person it chose?" Hicket asked, enthralled now by both the orb and its legend.

"Again, it is obscure. The young Montfort who found

it continues in the story and legend puts the orb in York soon after his journey to that place, but it was not a straight path. Many say that it came to a mathematician in Oxford on the river Isis, but I have heard it told that this scholar was also of the Montfort family. If this is true, then the orb would again return to York."

Robert took the orb from her and studied it, his expression solemn. "There were knights from York staying at Pynford."

She looked up at this young son who now towered over her. "There is one more thing. If the orb has any power other than the power to choose its own path, it is said to be a power to control time."

"Time?" It was Hicket who asked.

"We only know time as it moves forward, Hicket." Emeline was serious in this. "The bards say that in the presence of the orb, time has been known to move in different ways. To flow forward at a different pace or even perhaps to flow in reverse."

Robert refused to believe. "Time flowing backward? It could not happen." In the light of his recent visions though, this thought was frightening.

Hicket dismissed his skepticism. "It matters not. My interest is in how this orb came to be in our midst. If in truth it chooses its own path, then we have removed it from that path. We must return it now."

"No, Hicket. That is not so," Emeline protested. "If the orb does choose its own path, then it has come here for a purpose. It has chosen to be here."

"In this place at this time." It was the first time Mila had spoken and they turned to the girl that they had all but forgotten.

At this mention of time, though, Emeline became frightened. "Robert, I have been gone far too long. Rosalind's maidservant will be searching for me. Perhaps she has even returned to the manor. I must get back."

But when Robert looked toward the sun to see how far west it had traveled across the sky, he realized that in the time he was with his mother the sun had not moved at all.

He gazed down at the crystal that glowed from its innermost depths. "Mila?" He handed it to her. Now was not the time to decide what must become of the crystal. Instead they must find a way to keep Roland and Ricwyn safe. "Come, Mother. You must go back."

Again, Robert left Hicket and Mila alone with the horses and with the orb and led his mother back toward the orchard. Mila returned the orb to the beautifully carved box, and overhead, in the midst of a bright and sunny morning, an owl hooted.

CHAPTER 19
A Horse and a Boat

When Robert returned to the clearing he brought with him a sack of the ripe berries that grew inside the garden fence and some fish from the pond in the stream near the village.

"Very few, I fear." He apologized. "They know me well in the village and would recognize me. I could not spend much time near the fields."

The three moved to a clearing farther into the forest, built a small fire to roast his catch and settled down to a spare lunch.

"So what is it that we have learned?" Hicket asked at last.

"More than I had thought possible in such a short time," Robert told him. "Foremost, I know that Emeline is safe and that, for all his faults, Balian will most likely keep her so." Robert looked at Mila, sitting crossed legged in the grass devouring strawberries, a treat she was enjoying for the first time in her life. He knew that the meeting he had with his mother was because of her.

Then he listed the important facts for Hicket. "We know that Balian is planning to send a force to assist the invaders of Ireland who subdue the native people near Wexford. His efforts are most likely meant to gain prestige by aiding more powerful lords and also to increase his own lands, for the forces already there are acquiring lordship over the native population and colonizing their land.

"We know Balian plans to send Roland, an able steward, on this mission. The thoughts behind this could be twofold. First to help organize any lands his forces manage to gain, but second, perhaps, to remove Roland's careful oversight from Ricwyn. If Balian wants to establish his own control over the holdings here, he would want Roland out of his way."

It was not only Hicket who listened; Mila continued to devour berries, but she, too, took all this in.

Now Robert's brow creased in concern. "And more, we can assume that Balian hopes to keep his efforts secret from those lords to whom Ricwyn owes allegiance."

"Are they many?" Hicket asked.

"Many. Ricwyn is but a small holding, Balian a lord of little prestige. Many barons are above him in standing and he holds Ricwyn by their good grace. Under an oath of fealty, he owes those lords fully equipped knights in time of war and tithes, too. Sending a force to Ireland will reduce his ability to provide either."

"Gregory of Pynford is one of the lords Balian owes allegiance?"

"He is. And instead of asking Gregory's permission to undertake an excursion of this size, Balian keeps it from him. More, he takes me away from Pynford and from my duties there only to assist him in his secret venture."

"I can see how this reflects on your good name, Robert. You cannot join this force and still uphold your allegiance to Gregory."

"An allegiance that has already been broken, Hicket. I left Pynford of my own will."

"We left Pynford only yesterday, Robert. Surely Gregory will allow you a few days to mourn the death of your father."

"But if I return I must tell Gregory of Balian's plans. This will bring down the family of Ricwyn."

"Your family." Hicket considered the difficult choice Robert faced and they fell into silence.

Mila, who owed allegiance to no one, could not understand. She finished the last of the berries and wiped her stained fingers in the grass. "Why must you do one or the other?"

They looked over at her.

"I would not want to join forces with Balian. He does not seem trustworthy. But why return to Pynford? We have already chosen not to be there." The all-inclusive 'we' was not noticed by Robert, though it made Hicket smile.

Mila, as always, thought about what she would like

to do. "We may want to go to Ireland. Thomond said the land is beautiful. And if we were in Ireland, we might help Roland. It seems he would do well to have you near him, Robert."

"Yes, Roland would do well to have me with him, but I refuse to join Balian in this."

"I did not think of joining Balian's forces, only of going to Ireland." Mila seemed to see no difficulty in this.

"Across the sea?" Hicket asked.

"Thomond said it is not such a wide sea."

Hicket was amused by the way Mila's ignorance always stoked her enthusiasm. Mila would jump into anything. "Still, it is not a sea I should like to swim," he said.

"No!" The foolish sentiment annoyed her. "Of course we would not swim. We would need a boat. And we need another horse. We three and all of Robert's equipment are far too much for only two horses."

"A boat and another horse." Hicket shook his head.

Mila narrowed her eyes in thought. "Well, a horse is no problem. There are so many in the Ricwyn stable just now they will not miss one, not for a short time at least."

"So you will just slip into the manse unnoticed, as you do, and ride out on a charger?"

"Of course not, Hicket. But there must be a way. Robert is familiar with the stables. He knows the manner in which the squires there order their day."

Hicket realized she was serious. "Mila, they would hang you for stealing a horse."

"Only if we were caught." They were back to 'we' again. "And there must be boats that travel the sea to Ireland. Many of the bards who came to Pynford journeyed from across the sea."

Robert had listened to this banter with some amusement, but he could only listen so long. "God's bones, Mila, what would you have us do in Ireland?"

She shrugged. "Well, what will we do here?"

CHAPTER 20
To Steal a Horse

Stealing a horse was a new adventure for Robert and Hicket. In the end, Robert agreed to it only if the horse belonged to the manor of Ricwyn and therefore his family; the distinction made him feel as though he were simply borrowing the animal for his own use. But it posed a problem: because there were so many different horses in the stable at the manor now, they had no way of knowing which belonged to Ricwyn.

And their first thought, of course, was to take a horse from the stable. It might be done in the darkness of night when the stable was quiet. Ah, but then the manor gate would be closed and guarded. During the day, though, any horseman leaving the yard would be stopped and questioned.

Robert and Hicket were about to abandon the idea—knowing full well that abandonment was the wisest course—when Mila posed a different approach.

"Balian hunts?" she asked.

"Almost daily," Robert assured her. "It is the chief reason I fear discovery here in the Ricwyn forest."

"Then we can surely take a horse during the hunt." Mila spoke as if this were an easy task.

But again, it was not. "Balian and his men hunt together, Mila. One is seldom far from the others. Isolating a huntsman would be almost impossible. He would remain in earshot of so many others."

She thought again. "Do no riders leave the manor yard alone?" Now that was a valid consideration.

"Messengers." It was Hicket who said this. He looked at Robert. "The messenger who came to Pynford traveled alone."

"Yes," Robert agreed. "And because of the danger of thieves along the paths, messengers are given the swiftest of rides in the stable. Any horse of a messenger is sure to be worthy."

"And messengers travel by the route through Pynford Forest." Mila liked this idea.

"But we would not want to venture nearer Pynford." Hicket, too, was warming to the thought of a lone messenger on a wooded path. "There must be other solitary paths nearer Ricwyn, Robert. Paths a messenger would follow if sent to other destinations."

"Many." Robert at last thought this may be possible. It became more a challenge, a foolhardy game of wits, than a crime. And they must leave here now; the forest of

Ricwyn was too dangerous a place for them.

Eventually, the path Robert chose for the gambit was one that led east and south, away from Ricwyn and also from Pynford. They found a spot far enough beyond the village, too, so as not to risk discovery from any local. The question now was whether Balian's messengers were still frequenting these paths. By midafternoon, they had the answer. A man rode from the direction of Ricwyn traveling as fast as the rutted path and half-light of the overhanging trees allowed, and the three stood in concealed silence as he passed.

Mila was anxious for action, but Robert and Hicket wanted to be cautious. "Mila, we had to know if messengers do come this way," Hicket said. He stepped into the path and watched the man disappear.

Robert joined him. "I thought they must. There are many small holdings as you travel south toward the sea, manors that support one or two knights only. These would be the lords Balian would choose to join him in a secret venture for gain."

Hicket nodded. "Then we could hope for another rider soon."

Mila was with them on the path now. "We need only to stop him. Once off his horse, we will just take it and ride off."

"Mila, surely no man would just let you ride away with his horse," Robert scolded, his doubts about this venture resurfacing.

"Well, if he travels from Ricwyn, the horse most likely belongs to Balian. Its loss might not matter so very much to the rider."

"Perhaps we should just stop him and ask," suggested Hicket.

Mila, though, was serious. "Hicket, that would be foolish. No, I'll stop him and ask for help."

The thought of a messenger stopping on a heavily wooded path to aid a scruffy peasant provided Hicket further amusement. "Help for what?"

"Wait, Hicket." She disappeared into the undergrowth only to appear in a short time wearing a beautiful soft cloak and carrying a glowing crystal orb.

She bowed slightly. "Please, sir, I must get this to Ricwyn. But no one must know. My arrival must be secret."

Hicket looked at Robert. They both laughed.

But Mila was sincere. "Please, good sir, will you turn on the path and take me back to Ricwyn?" She was well pleased with her ruse until the hoot of an owl gave her pause. Suddenly she grew cold and shivered as she searched for the bird in the overhanging branches.

It was only a short time before another lone rider from the direction Ricwyn traveled the path, but now their well laid plan turned around unexpectedly.

First, the rider came at a murderous pace, almost running into Mila as she stood in the center of the narrow path. Then, on seeing the orb, the rider's first thought was not to dismount and help but to draw a knife and lean forward to strike at her and steal the crystal. His decision took but an instant, his action was swift. But as he unsheathed his knife a large owl swooped down from a branch above his head, its feather wing tips brushing his face. It startled him.

Robert was first into the clearing. As the rider jerked backward, Robert grabbed at the hand readied to strike the blow, twisting the arm backward, dismounting the man, throwing him to the ground. At almost the same moment, Hicket reached for Mila and pulled her to safety.

In seconds the three were mounted and away, leading a rather nice looking chestnut stallion and leaving behind a dazed rider with a message far different than the one he had been sent to deliver. His new tale was of a ball of sun held in the hands of a girl who wore a cloak spun of moonlight; of a monstrous bird of prey plunging from the sky; and of a giant knight who pulled him from his saddle and threw him to the ground.

It was a tale that grew more fantastic with each telling.

CHAPTER 21
A Journey West

They stopped in a clearing to regroup. Mila dismounted first, eager to admire the sleek, well-tended animal they had 'captured'. "Lovely," in her opinion. She circled the horse. "Lovely."

Robert examined the stallion carefully. Young but not too young, obviously well trained, large and sturdy. "Hicket's, I should think."

Mila was about to protest, but yielded instantly when she saw the broad smile appear on Hicket's disfigured face. "Hicket's then," she agreed. "And he must have a name worthy of his size."

"Alduin, then," Hicket decided, mimicking Mila's tone. "It would be good to name him for a dragon."

"A dragon?" Mila's eyes opened in horror. "Have you seen this dragon?"

"It's a tale told by firelight, Mila," Hicket assured her. "Still, a good name."

"Alduin, then." She repeated the name as she reached up to stroke the hind quarter of the stallion. "But what have we here?"

A leather pouch was fastened in place almost under the saddle, concealed from any but the most observant. Hicket pulled at pouch until Mila drew the karambit from her belt and cut the bands that held it in place. He untied woven leather strands at the top of the pouch, pulled it open and turned it upside down. Four gold coins spilled onto the ground.

"Lovelier and lovelier." Mila gathered them up and held them out for inspection.

"And a message." Hicket drew a folded parchment from the bottom of the pouch. The folds were intricate, the parchment thin, as if scraped many times. Together the fragile nature of the scraped parchment and its rough surface made the writing difficult to decipher.

Robert took it from Hicket and studied the words. "We need time to read this. We should travel first. If the gold and this message were from Balian, he will surely send men to search for us. It would be good to be far from Ricwyn by nightfall."

Hicket looked down the path in the opposite direction from where they had come: east and south, away from Ricwyn. "This way, then."

But Robert disagreed. "If we are to cross to Ireland we would do better to travel west."

Mila turned and looked back up the path. "Back toward

Ricwyn? Surely that would not be wise."

"Not due west but west more to the south, leaving a wide distance between our route and all Ricwyn land."

"Do you know these parts well, Robert?" Hicket asked.

"As a young boy I traveled many of the routes south with my father. Our ties with the manors there are of long standing. Still, if we are to cross to Ireland we must go farther west, across the embankment of Offa's Dyke and through the hills beyond it before we reach the sea. My father considered this rough land." Robert stopped here, reconsidering. "Once there, we may travel to the coast and beyond by water. In some parts this is possible."

"Roland spoke of the River Usk," Hicket remembered.

"I only know that beyond Offa's Dyke the land is mountainous and the rivers are swift. Often, the language of the people differs, too. But as we near the coast we may find this river will provide ports for ships."

"You mean we would travel on a river by boat?" Mila, who planned her life in hours, truly never more than the span of a day, had not given serious thought to an actual journey to Ireland. She was thrilled by such an adventure.

In truth, Robert, too, had not thought of it in a practical way. If he had taken the time to do this, he would never have agreed to so reckless a venture. But they were in the midst of it now. "This is something we must sort as we go," he said, his eyes fixed on the path ahead. "Our first goal must be to travel far from Ricwyn. We will go south now. Soon this path will cross with others and we will choose one leading west."

Hicket helped Mila onto Luagor, mounted the stallion Alduin and took the reins of both horses. "I'll lead you forward until you are comfortable riding. It will take time to learn this."

As she struggled to stay atop Luagor, she realized the truth of his words. But she would learn. After this day's work, she realized riding a horse and handling a knife would become two of the most important skills in her new universe.

CHAPTER 22
Plotting in a Leafy Wood

Offa's Dyke. The name gave Mila chills. A wall separating this land from the rough land to the west, wherever west was.

She trotted along behind Hicket and Alduin for what seemed hours, legs tensed against the saddle, hanging on to anything that held her in place. Luagor was a gentle palfrey and the steady pace they kept, the regular motion, made it easier. Daydreams of towering walls and 'rough land' beyond were the best antidote to an uncomfortable ride: Offa's dyke; a port on a swift river; mariners and a boat.

After a time they turned onto a crossing path that put the afternoon sun in her eyes. They skirted some small villages, but only a few minstrels and a man in monks' robes riding a donkey passed them on that route and they rarely slowed the pace.

Toward evening they entered the fields of a large village

with a church spire reaching higher into the sky than any structure Mila had ever seen. People streaming from the town told them it was market day, which Robert held to be good luck; the closing stalls would be the best place to secure the food they needed. But as they left the path and drew up near a slow moving stream, his first thought was of the note that the messenger carried.

They dismounted and he spread the thin parchment open, reading the words slowly, carefully. Hicket, standing next to him, also read the message. After a time Robert raised his head and stared away into some unknown distance, his thoughts far away from the clearing. Soon Hicket, too, looked up and away.

"What? What?" Mila was growing more anxious.

Hicket looked down at her. "It is what we feared—and worse than we feared. Balian has gathered a very large force, much larger than were at the manse, and they are prepared to leave for Ireland immediately. He sends this money to Newport to secure boats for the journey." He paused, looked over at his friend. "Robert?"

"I have too many thoughts swirling about, Hicket. Where did Balian secure so many men? For a force this size he must have pulled knights from every manor within the influence of Ricwyn. And gathered soldiers for hire, too. And disgruntled men from Ireland like those that Mila saw." He was silent for a moment. "But how will he manage this force without the help of stronger men like Gregory of Pynford?"

Robert lowered his head, pondering the consequences of Balian's deceit. "More, when Gregory discovers the deceit, how will Balian defend his actions? I worry about the fate of Lady Emeline and of my brother Roland. There are others, too, who will bear the pain. My sisters married into families that Balian may have involved in this action. If it collapses, they will be punished."

Mila was beginning to understand the web of fealties that maintained the feudal order and the consequences of defying them.

"Is there nothing we can do, Robert?" Hicket asked.

"We might do something," Mila suggested.

"The three of us? What? Turn an army of men?" Robert scoffed at her. "God's bones, Mila, grow up." He turned away.

She was stung by the rebuke, smitten like a young pup struck by a harsh and heavy hand. Feeling her pain, Hicket reached out and touched her shoulder, but he said nothing. She turned her back to them and walked into a nearby clump of trees. Robert and Hicket were silent for some time, a time that slowed with them.

Robert was reacting, but Hicket, who viewed the situation from a greater distance, was able to consider it more carefully. "In truth, Robert, we must not turn an entire army but only a man. We need only disrupt the plans of Balian."

At last Robert looked toward his friend. "A man with an army."

"But only one man."

Hicket turned to Mila, who had emerged from the trees and slowly, haltingly returned to the clearing. Her inexperience with these matters made her view the problem in a different way, but she too saw that Balian was the key.

Yes, he was the key. And there seemed to be very few outcomes possible. "Hicket, what would be best for the family of Ricwyn? Would it be for them to stop Balian from sending this army to Ireland now, to stop him by informing more powerful lords like Gregory of his actions? Would they stop Balian and forgive the family? What if these lords were told of his plans?" She stared up at him. "Or, if Balian does send this force to Ireland, what would be the best result then? Would it be best if he failed in his mission to secure land and gain power, or best if he had great success? What would happen then?" Each of these outcomes seemed possible to her, but she didn't know which might be best. And there might be other choices.

At last Robert was listening.

It was Hicket, though, who addressed her logic. "Each of those paths is possible, Mila." He considered them and also if there might be other choices. "In truth, I can think of no other."

"Then which is the best?"

Hicket considered this. "The first seems impossible. Balian's plans are too far along. How could we possibly inform Gregory at Pynford and hope he might react in time to stop Balian now?"

Robert joined them at last. "No." He shook his head. "We left Pynford without even telling Gregory we were going. How could we expect him to believe this news coming from us?"

"And, by the time he discovered it to be true, it would be far too late," Hicket agreed.

"It is far too late already." Robert still shook his head slowly.

But Mila had no time for regret; she took the practical approach. "Then Balian's force must go to Ireland, because if it were to remain here, there could be no good coming from that." She paused. "So what if it did go to Ireland and it failed?"

Robert had no hesitation on this. "No good would come from that, Mila. I have no regard for Balian, but surely he would suffer both at the hands of the lords he coerced into joining him in a losing adventure and those he disobeyed by not informing them of his plan. This would ruin the entire family."

"But if his plan is successful?"

Hicket gave this thought. "It may result in the lord of Ricwyn becoming much more powerful, a lord too wealthy and powerful for others to contest."

"Then that is the only choice." Mila spoke with authority.

"Choice?" Hicket asked. "What choice do we have in this?"

"We can insure that Roland will be successful."

"We can?" Hicket laughed. "Good that we can do this. Do you have your knife with you, Mila? Should I draw my sword now?"

"But surely Balian felt that Robert would make a difference. He sent to Pynford for Robert to return to Ricwyn so that he could join Roland."

"He did." Hicket began to see some sense in this. "And we know the beginning of Balian's plan, Robert. We know the number of his forces, where he plans to depart, where he hopes to land in Ireland. We even have money to secure a boat." He paused, thought about what they might do. "We may be able to do very little, but you did feel that you would like to go with Roland, if only to insure his own safety."

Mila was feeling better. "And, after all, going to Ireland doesn't change our plans at all."

Robert's only reaction was, "God's bones." But he had no better idea. Staying here remained the least attractive of any actions.

CHAPTER 23
Beyond Offa's Dyke

Robert thought they were far enough from Ricwyn to enter the village and buy food, but the choice of which of them might do this was difficult. The three together were too odd a collection to be forgotten. Alone, Robert might still be within the boundaries of manors known to his family; Hicket, with his disfigured face, was certain to be remembered; and a young girl traveling on her own was sure to raise questions. In the end, it was Robert who ventured forth.

"A dashing knight-errant will be quickly accepted," Hicket teased, and then spent the time Robert was away explaining 'errant' to Mila, filling her with bards' tales of knights wandering the countryside in search of adventure.

When Robert returned with loaves of bread, a sack of meats, dried fruit and a small cask of ale, the smell that wafted about him made Mila realize just how hungry she was. But instead of eating and resting, he insisted on riding again until they were far enough away from the village to feel safe. It was dark and riding had become difficult when they left the path to finally eat and rest; Mila was thankful for both. But the next day brought more of the same, traveling west over a landscape that became increasingly steep and more difficult to maneuver.

The mysterious dyke of Offa that had seeped into Mila's daydreams proved to be only a broad ditch and a crumbling embankment that briefly hindered their crossing; over time countless riders had smoothed an easy passageway through the barrier. Mila, concentrating on riding Luagor without Hicket holding the reins, barely noticed it, but soon realized that the hills on the far side were even more rugged, their route often narrowing into a steep and rocky climb and then plunging in a more dangerous descent. Keeping her seat through the horse's slips and stumbles took all her concentration. It was the few times when she did tumble to the ground that she realized her good fortune, for each time, Robert turned back to help her.

At last, as they crested a hill, they saw a stone tower keep encircled by a wall and protective earthworks overlooking a swift flowing river, the River Usk; below the tower there was a village bordering the river. Here they turned southward to follow the river valley, and their journey became easier, the path smoother along the banks.

Another town on the Usk marked an entrance to a port, a town that Balian had mentioned as the place selected to begin the sea journey of his force. Robert had heard of the settlement before and knew it as the old Roman legion town of Caerleon. Many of the buildings here were of smooth stone, much of it taken from the ruins of the once impressive Roman buildings and baths.

At first, Mila didn't understand the way one civilization might be built from the ruins of an earlier one, but the stone in the tower keep had held a fascination for her and she hung on Hicket's words as he explained the changes that came with the passage of time. "Those that came before leave their work to benefit us now, as we will for those that come after," he concluded. "History and posterity."

Mila twitched her head to one side. In the kitchen at Pynford she had listened to and absorbed much of the constant hum at her back, but she had never really thought about things beyond the everyday. This was a thought beyond. "Time gone by and time ahead, too? Why do you know about that, Hicket?"

"We study the past to understand the present, Mila. It helps us to not repeat mistakes made by earlier generations."

"And the people who will come after us. Do you know about them, too?"

Suddenly Robert interrupted. "Can we see into the future? Don't be daft, Mila." His tone was harsher than he intended because in the past few days his unshakeable belief in only one possible course for the flowing of time, his disdain for the foolish idea of seeing the future, had been undermined by his senses.

Hicket took his harsh words only as Robert being upset by circumstances. He smiled at Mila but fell silent. Still, the question hung in her mind. She thought about the passage of time.

Mostly, though, she was fascinated by the market town itself. Teaming streets were lined with houses; stalls sold goods of the like she had never seen. Cloth, some brightly colored and some soft as her cloak, was offered by many merchants. Fish in sizes and shapes she had never known in the kitchens at Pynford roasted on open fires, scenting the air. Butchers and bakers and even jewelers proffered their goods as they passed.

Both Hicket and Robert were amused by her astonishment and wonder, so much so that they further amused themselves by indulging her. She soon had a new tunic and belt, stockings and even leather shoes.

"Lovely," said Hicket, admiring her in her new finery.

But Robert could never be more than brutally honest and his praise was more subtle. "Mila, you look like a normal young girl." Whatever that meant.

Mila took it as praise. She was too overwhelmed to do otherwise. She wore a tunic that no one had ever worn before and new shoes of leather. She had a horse to ride and, hidden in the depths of a soft cloak, she carried a glowing treasure that Lady Emeline believed held secret powers. More than all of this, she had become a friend and companion of Robert de Ricwyn. Perhaps this last wasn't quite true yet, but thus far she had served him well and he was grateful. His favor would grow and his manner toward her soften, she was sure of it.

CHAPTER 24
Crossing the Sea

Only a short distance downstream below Caerleon, at a place called Newport, the river opened into a wide stretch of water. It was a bright summer morning when they arrived and boats of all sizes bobbed on the gentle waves and lined the low banks south of the bustling town.

Some of the boats were small and could be handled by just a few men using paddles—oars, Hicket called them. Many of these smaller boats were filled with piles of pink or grey fish.

Other boats were huge, bigger than a cottage, and had a sail at the center that filled with wind to push the boat forward. Many of these larger boats had sides that curved into points at both ends, just as most of the smaller boats had. For some reason, these were called cogs. Still many more of the large ships had towering flat fronts and backs and were called hulks. Hulks were used by merchants to transport goods across the seas, and along the waterfront many were being loaded with barrels and crates, while just as many more were being unloaded.

The entire bank was busy and loud and smelled of sea air and salt water and even the rare spices Mila knew from the kitchen at Pynford. The entire scene was very different from anything Mila had ever experienced.

It was here that Robert and Hicket planned to secure a boat to take them to Ireland, and suddenly Mila was frightened with the prospect of actually crossing the sea. She found her eyes filling with tears and had to hang her head to hide wet cheeks. As Robert strode ahead to survey the different boats assembled along the embankment, Hicket stayed with her and put his arm around her shoulders.

"All will be fine, Mila. It is but a short journey." He smiled down at her, crinkling the angry red skin under his blind eye.

Robert returned with the news that a large military expedition to Ireland was expected and many of the ships here had gathered for the journey. Crates of weapons were already stored in the large buildings along the shore of the port. He was staggered by the scale of the planned expedition.

"Balian has been preparing for this for a very long time. I am appalled by his ruthless scheme, but I am impressed by this organization." His eyes narrowed. "I must wonder, Hicket, if he could have conceived this on his own."

"If not, Robert, who might have joined him in this?" Hicket asked.

"Joined him?" The words gave Robert pause. "Yes, perhaps we have given Balian more credit than he deserves. Perhaps we should think of this in another way. Might someone have employed him? This expedition would take much more gold than the few coins we took from the messenger. How could Balian have acquired so much money?" He paused, pondered. "Hicket, I believe there is someone else behind this, someone far greater than the new lord of Ricwyn. Balian is but a cog in the wheel." Robert seethed. "Balian has put our family fortunes at risk for the sake of joining with a more powerful Lord."

Mila's fear of a sea journey faded, overcome by another fear fostered by the tone in Robert's voice. When he again sank into the depths of his thought, she looked toward Hicket for an explanation.

Hicket, too, was uneasy. "We have run away from Pynford, Mila, disavowing our sworn allegiance to Gregory. The death of Edmund and the request of Balian for Robert to return to Ricwyn could have provided cover for leaving Pynford, but we refused the excuse of going to Ricwyn and disobeyed Balian, too. Now we find that Balian must have the protection of a much greater lord, one certainly more powerful than Gregory. So you see, we have gained yet another foe, this one of great wealth."

Mila considered their predicament for only a moment. Her reaction was not what Hicket would have expected from a young girl beset by threats from powerful lords. Instead it was the reaction of an inconsequential scullery, a child whose daily life in the kitchens had been made secure only by avoiding confrontation.

Her head tilted to one side; she was thinking now of a safe place to hide. "So how far across the sea is this Ireland? And how big is it?"

Despite the peril of their situation, Hicket, and then Robert, too, laughed.

In the end, it was not a ship readied to carry arms that bore them across the sea, but the ship of a merchant carrying wine to the markets created by the invading English lords who had already established fiefdoms in and around Wexford. The merchant-sailor who owned the ship was an old man with skin darker than the leather of Mila's new shoes. His tattered tunic hung loose about his shoulders but was fastened tightly at his waist and hips, as were the stockings on his bowed legs.

He had come from Bordeaux and most of the large barrels of his shipment had been downloaded here in Newport; the cargo of his hulk was reduced to a small fraction of what it could carry. Half a gold coin persuaded him to take aboard this powerful knight, his scarred companion and the young servant girl they had with them.

At first Mila was terrified by the size of this ship, one of the bigger vessels with a flat front and back. She had barely become accustomed to crossing bridges and now she was about to take a journey across an expanse of water with no far shore in sight. "If we can't see the land, how will we get there? How can he know where we are going?" she asked Hicket.

"Those that sail the sea have ways," he assured her, but she could not be convinced.

As they boarded the ship, men continued to upload provisions for the journey and the merchant was on guard, shouting orders; but once they were ready to sail, he had idle time while they awaited the tide. Hicket, who gauged Mila's fear, took her to stand with the old man at the top of a raised platform at the rear of the ship. From there they could look across the deck and out across the widening water beyond.

"This will be an easy crossing, child," the sailor told them, pleased to have an audience for his knowledge. "But first we must await the tide."

"Tide?" Mila asked.

"Aye, the rise of the water coming in from the sea." He nodded and smiled a wise old smile. "You see, the seas swell and fall in rhythm. It is different in every place and in every season, but just here the rise will come on soon."

Now the idea of a sea rising and falling was frightening

to her. It gave this unending expanse of water breath—a seething, overpowering life of its own.

But not so the old sailor: the sea was his life and he had more to tell. "It is a good thing. In this warm season the flow of water from the River Usk is low, so we must wait for the incoming water to be high before we can clear the port."

Wide eyed, Mila hung on his words. "So sometimes the river has more water?"

"Aye. I have seen it flow so full it overruns its banks. That is in the cooler season."

"If we have many weeks of rain, Mila, a river will flood," Hicket explained.

"Like when I put too much water into my sink." That made sense.

The old man laughed at this. "Just so, only 'tis God that does the putting here. Now, when we leave, we sail west down the coast, hugging the shore. Then we turn north into more open water. But still we keep this coast in sight. Wise to sail north a bit to keep the channel to the open sea far south of us, for that channel can rage."

"The channel?" Mila pictured the rage of a monstrous sea beast.

"Aye. The open water between here and the Wexford coast is just a small sea. It opens to a large ocean at two ends, one north and one south. Both of these openings are narrow. At times water flows in from the channel at the south and sweeps north, and at times 'tis just the other way around. When water is pushed in from one side or 'tother, the flow can be swift near the narrow openings. The wind that pushes it makes waves that can be monstrous. 'Tis a longer route, sailing north along the coast and then across the wider part of this sea, but it will be a safer one." He paused to look up at the sky. "Still, today I see no trouble. The sky is clear and the winds are gentle. With luck, we might have you there tomorrow."

"So you see, Mila, we are in luck," Hicket assured her.

"Aye, no summer storms today," the old man agreed. "If the sky stays clear, you can stay up here all through the journey."

Which would be a blessing; the areas below the deck were dark and foul.

But then the old man's expression turned quizzical. "Look, the sun has already shifted and the tide comes swiftly." He gazed up at the sky and his brow furrowed. "There can be no storm on the sea or we would feel the change. And still, the tide, it rises so fast. I have never seen it rise so swiftly." He left them suddenly to see to the departure.

"Look, the sun shifts fast across the sky, Mila, and the tide comes swiftly," Hicket repeated. He, too, appeared puzzled.

Just then an owl hooted, a rare sound in a busy port on a bright summer day. Mila's eyes rose to the top of the bar that held the sail. The owl perched there, its head swiveling quickly, first facing out to sea, then across the town and then turning to look toward the sea again, as if it were wary and eager to be away. Following the direction of the owl's gaze from her place on the raised deck of the ship Mila could see a contingent of men on horseback entering the upper gate of the town.

Suddenly the ship lurched forward, and Mila lost her footing. As she struggled to stand upright, the owl's head shifted downward and its steady gaze locked onto her eyes, but it was silent.

IRELAND IN THE REIGN OF KING HENRY III

CHAPTER 25
Wexford and Beyond

The harbor they entered on the next morning was different from the land of steep hills they had left, but it was not surrounded by the green fields and sparkling clear waters of Thomond's memory. Instead, the shore here was flat and muddy and filled with too many birds, more birds than Mila had ever seen in one place. Loud calling birds shattered the lulling pattern of waves lapping against the side of the creaking ship, a sound that she had become accustomed to over the quiet night. Odd bits of land seemed to rise out of the water, too, or in places, out of an expanse of mud, making much of the shoreline appear not quite land or sea.

The town they sought was on the far side of this misty shore/lake in a place just south of where a river flowed out into the broader waters. It was surrounded by a stone wall and edged with the same bustle of boats as the harbor they left, large boats and small, loading and unloading. The cargo their own ship carried, though, was one of importance and the wine merchant well known. Soon a smaller vessel approached, pull ropes were exchanged and their boat lurched forward and turned into a sudden halt. Mila lost her footing again, but this time she was grateful for it because now all motion ceased. She jumped up and followed on the heels of Robert and Hicket as they gathered the horses, and shortly she walked onto the succor of solid land.

They found themselves in a market town much like the one they had left, the goods in the stands almost all the same. The sounds that flowed past Mila, though, were different. Some people spoke the same sharp words she did, some the softer tones of Robert and Hicket. But many spoke words she had never heard before, not at Pynford or even in the places along their journey. Most of the men behind the stalls seemed to not mind these many different words and shifted their own words to match. But the jumble of words, the changing pitch and pattern, heightened the confusion of the busy market.

Robert was anxious to escape the busy streets and seek shelter in quieter quarters, "Some place we can stay while we discover the exact plans of Balian's invading force." They bought bread and ale, cheeses and other provisions from stalls along a street that led out of the town and left the port to ride west into the late morning sun. Just north of the town they were forced to ride off the main road to avoid Carrick Castle, a stronghold built by the invaders almost a century before to protect the mouth of the river.

As the path climbed away from the sea, the land grew more like the land Thomond remembered, a country of green hills and sparkling blue lakes and streams. At first, they passed manor houses much like those Mila saw before they sailed, large houses surrounded by walls and fields and the cottages of those who worked the land. But in a short time, the manor houses became less frequent and the cottages of workers were farther scattered with many neglected or even in ruin.

When the sun was high in a brilliant blue sky and she had grown hot, hungry and tired, they came across one of these ramshackle dwellings near a fork in the path. A man in the foreyard worked on a large, wooden handled scythe, sharpening the blade on a wheel that spun unevenly. Robert dismounted and approached him.

After but a short greeting, Robert said in a friendly voice, "The path forks. Might you tell us which is the main route?"

The man spoke without slowing the wheel or stopping his work, "Main road goes to your left." His words were different than those she was accustomed to hearing, but he indicated the direction with his left hand, while still grasping the scythe in his right, so Mila had a better idea of his words.

"And the other?" Robert asked, shifting his own words to reflect the sound of the man's.

The man finally lifted the scythe from the wheel and his gaze shifted toward the steeper path that curved down into overhanging trees. "'Tis the way to the old manor of Rosskinross." He studied Robert for a moment, then Hicket and finally Mila. Whatever he saw was not to his liking; he lowered his head and pressed the scythe to the wheel again.

"Does anyone live there?" Robert asked.

The man lifted the scythe from the spinning stone and looked up again.

"At Rosskinross? Does anyone live there?" Robert repeated.

The wheel spun, but the man stared at Robert. "And who is it that asks?"

"No one of authority." Robert's tone was soft, reassuring. "We are strangers in this country and simply seek a place we might rest."

The man eyed the armor and weapons they carried, judged the size of the mighty grey charger, Abatos, the muscles of the swift Alduin and even Mila's large and steady mount, Luagor. "Ye bear arms," was all he said, but his tone held more.

"The arms of one lone knight and his companions."

"Aye." His tone grew sarcastic. "To my knowledge, knights serve sires. Who be yours?"

"In truth, sir, I answer to no one. We travel freely and

seek only a place to shelter."

"Aye, and hope someone is there who will welcome you at Rosskinross."

Hicket swung to the ground and approached the man. "We grow weary," he said in a tone that was naturally softer than Robert's. "Might we stop there to rest for a short time?"

The man caught Hicket's gaze with his own, held it for a time. "It is not my business to stop you." Suddenly his wheel spun faster and sparks flew as he returned the scythe to its rim.

Sensing this was an end to all conversation, Hicket mounted Alduin and shrugged. Robert answered Hicket's shrug with another, mounted Abatos and turned toward the steeper path, with Mila urging Luagor forward to follow.

IRELAND IN THE REIGN OF KING JOHN LACKLAND

CHAPTER 26
The Deserted Manor of Rosskinross

Within a short distance the descent became narrow and steep and the twisting path dimmed under the cover of overhanging trees, many with branches hanging so low Robert and Hicket were forced to hunch forward over the necks of their horses to avoid them. Progress was slow and the darkness of the path dulled their sight, leaving them ill prepared for the burst of light at its end. Blinking in its sudden intensity, Luagor stumbled into the back of Alduin and Mila and Hicket struggled for a moment to keep their seats.

All three came to a halt, allowing their eyes to gradually adjust to the brilliant sunshine and now were again overpowered, this time by the beauty of the scene that spread before them. They were on the shore of a silver lake; almost at their feet, sparkling water shimmered against a ribbon of grass as green as any Thomond had conjured. The water, the land and the clear blue sky that rose above them dazzled them into silence.

Taken by surprise as she was, the scene should have filled Mila's senses, stopped all other thought for some time. But something more startling slowly pushed the vision to the background.

Silence. Unnerving silence.

No birds called, no wind rustled in the treetops. No fish jumped and plopped back into the glass surface of the water; no beetles burrowed; no flies buzzed. Silence.

Luagor, Abatos, even the often skittish Alduin held taught, ears up, tails down, hooves firmly planted. Unmoving. Silent.

It seemed as if all the world had stopped, held its breath. One beat, two. Silence.

And then, slowly, carefully, it breathed again. The air was filled with familiar sounds of a summer lake.

Robert was first to recover. He looked to the right along the shore and then raised his hand, pointing to the manor house they expected to see. It stood on a slight rise above deserted water meadows that circled that far edge of the large lake. A broad, well-worn path led through the grasses of the shore and the tall grasses and they turned to follow it.

As they approached the manor, they were impressed by the height of the wall that surrounded it, a wall of timber paling atop a broad stone base. A sturdy gate protected the inner yard, but it stood opened and unguarded.

Inside the wall, the courtyard was much what Mila had come to expect of manor houses. There was a long row of stables to the far side and a kitchen protected by a low walled garden on the side near the lake. Here, another gate in the wall led to the shore, but it, too, was opened wide to all comers. As she looked through this gate, she could see a cluster of small cottages farther along the shore, a steeple in its midst, and large cultivated fields stretching away from the village edge. A rocky hillside at the back of the village curved to surround the fields, and a stream rushed down its slope. In the far distance, the hillside was dotted with sheep—sheep, but no people.

The manor house was built closer to the ground than the manor at Ricwyn, seemingly having no storage cellar under the main floor, and though well proportioned, it was less grand, rougher. Windows were few, small and deeply set; in contrast, the entry door was large but barred, the bars appearing to be a recent addition.

Within the kitchen wall, chickens scratched the earth and a rookery was alive with the busy coming and going of birds; but no scullery maid plodded the path bearing a tub of water, no cook shouted orders, no man tended the neat rows of plantings. The stables held no horses and no boys bustled about with brooms and brushes. In the forecourt, no squires crossed wooden swords and no elder servants gossiped at the well. There were no people.

Hicket turned to Robert, but he could offer no insight.

"Might they be within?" Hicket suggested.

At this, Robert rode toward the manor door, dismounted and strode up the few stone steps to examine the sturdy iron bars that protected the entry. He pulled at a ring near the latch, half expecting it to yield, but it held fast.

Hicket rode toward the stable, then along the front wall and back to where Robert stood at the top of the steps to the door. "Surely if anyone is about, they must know that we are here, Robert."

"But there must be someone here." Robert scanned the courtyard, looked toward the kitchen. "The yard is swept clean. The stables, the garden—all is in good order here. There are no signs of the family or the servants making a hasty departure."

"The stable is large," Hicket said thoughtfully. "Rosskinross must keep many horses, which speaks of many men."

"But none here." Robert called out now, trying to rouse someone within the house. He circled toward the kitchen and back along the garden wall then called out again.

Clearly both Robert and Hicket were astounded. Mila, too, thought it strange, but she was very hungry.

"Surely they must know we come in peace." Robert and Hicket turned toward her. "What threat could we be?"

Hicket saw the logic in this. "That much is true, Robert. Anyone here must know we pose no threat to them. We travel alone and, though we carry weapons, we bear no arms."

"Could we at least stop here to eat?" Mila's priorities never faltered.

"Not here in the courtyard." Robert's glance again scanned the empty stable. "Until we know what happened to the people who belong to this manor, we will be safer on open ground."

He mounted Abatos and led them back through the main gate and toward the lakeshore. In a shaded thicket overlooking an island thick with trees that rose from the center of the water, Robert and Hicket tended the horses and Mila prepared a meal from the provisions they bought in Wexford.

Birds flew between the treetops, bees buzzed among wild flowers and a few lazy fish broke the lake surface to make half-hearted attempts at water spiders, causing ripples that spread gently outward in slow moving concentric rings. Mila sat in the midst of fresh bread and cheeses and dried meats and dreamed of living here—forever perhaps. With Robert at her side and Hicket here too, as the good friend he was. They would all be so happy in this place.

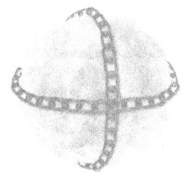

CHAPTER 27
The Bewitching Maeve

The boat appeared from around the far side of the island. It might have come from the island itself or from the opposite shore of the lake, from some part of the shore hidden from sight by the island; there was no way to know. Either way, it posed little threat. It was a small boat and, as it approached, they could see that it held only three men. No wait, two men and a woman. The men at each end were elderly, grey bearded, but they rowed in practiced unison; the woman at the center stood unmoving, practiced, too, and unfazed by the boat's gentle rocking.

Slowly, carefully, the men brought the boat across the water, drew near to them and then turned it, so that the side almost touched the shore, but not so near that it scraped the lake bottom. Then, by dropping their oars deeper, they managed to hold it in place against the slight motion of incoming waves. By this time the woman had turned toward the shore, her face set into frown of curiosity, even wonder, as she studied the three travelers. Robert and Hicket rose and walked closer to the shore, but Mila only squared her shoulders and sat taller. Her reaction was immediate. She would not like this woman who had so easily intruded into her dream. Though the boat rocked gently, she stood perfectly still as she studied Robert and his disfigured companion Hicket; she was far too composed, too serene, too haughty. More, with lovely white skin, a cloud of golden red curls and eyes as blue as the sky above the lake, she was too beautiful. Far too beautiful.

When she spoke, it was first in the strange language that Mila heard since they came to this land; but as soon as Robert replied, the woman—maiden, really, for her age could not be so very much more than Mila's own—spoke again using their own tongue.

"You do not speak as we do," she said. "You come from across the sea, then?" In this tongue, her words were lilting, her voice as soft as the red gold hair that blew away from her face in the breeze.

"We arrived in Wexford only a short time ago," Robert answered as she focused on him.

"You have traveled here from Wexford on the coast?" She tilted her head to one side, her frown increasing.

"Our ship landed there and we rode inland."

She held his gaze as if gravely assessing the honesty of his words. "Wexford is distant. I know only of the stronghold of Carrick that was built there by the invaders."

Her eyes misted at the thought of it. "Invaders from across the sea come to take over our land, to steal our cattle and our sheep, to build market towns with walls to sell the stuff of our labor to others and grow rich on the sweat of our brow."

Robert had no answer he wanted to make so stood silent as she scrutinized him.

Her eyes narrowed into an ill-natured scowl that should have disfigured her features but, instead, only made their perfect symmetry more alluring. "They come to Rosskinross now and will take this land, too."

"In truth, we are not part of the forces that invade your land. If we had a purpose, it would be only to…" what? What were they hoping to accomplish here in this strange land? Robert searched for an explanation, but found none. His eventual response was feeble, only "Our purpose is not that."

"But you have been traveling through my country for many days and you come here. Why is it?"

Hicket began to speak, to insist that they had arrived only earlier in the same day, but Robert put up his hand to still his friend.

Her eyes swept over Hicket and then fastened again on Robert. "So you are not with them, the men who come from across the sea? The men who fight the ceithern and take our land?"

"We are only travelers. We bear your people no ill will."

She looked toward Mila, as if trying to fathom all the

elements of the strange trio that had wandered into her domain, and quickly surveyed the remnants of the meal they had been eating.

"You have fresh bread and ale."

Hicket began the tale of buying provisions in Wexford, but as her penetrating blue eyes fixed on his, he realized that Wexford really was far distant and any bread from the coast should not be fresh. Puzzled, he grew silent.

Her gaze again shifted to Robert. "Your horse is strong and you carry armor. You are a knight, then?"

Robert only nodded.

"But you are not with the invaders? You do not come here to take our land?"

"That was never our intention. We have no desire to possess land. We are here in peace."

"I have no reason to trust you, Sir...?"

"Robert. I am Robert de Ricwyn. My companion is Hicket. And this is Mila." His hand gestured for Mila to stand and come forward, but she was having none of it. She sat in stony silence.

The girl looked toward the man at the front of the boat and he nodded. She then assumed what Mila came to call her haughty demeanor and spoke with the authority of a lord of the manor. "I am Maeve. Rosskinross is the home of my family. I have no reason to trust you, Sir Robert, but also no reason to doubt you. If you would come to stay at Rosskinross for a time, we would offer you lodging. It is our way. But these are difficult times, so in return you must trust us to stable your horses and store your armor."

Robert nodded, a smile softening the gesture.

"I will meet you in the courtyard." With that, she turned toward the front of the boat; the men turned it deftly with two powerful strokes and it slid away across the water leaving a wake.

Robert seemed transfixed as he watched the boat recede into the distance.

Mila did not like this, not at all. She rose and stared at the girl in the boat, her manner growing more hostile each time she witnessed a sweep of the oars. In the trees above her head an owl hooted.

CHAPTER 28
Enigma in Time

They were hiding, many in the trees along the far shore and more on the island. They had taken shelter when they were warned of three horsemen entering the path that led to Rosskinross, but now they returned to the work in the fields and the chores in the manse: women, children, and old men spilled into the streets of the village and the yard of the manor. In the midst of this unexpected bustle, Maeve awaited them in the forecourt.

After surveying the people emerging from the trees from atop Abatos, Robert was first to speak, asking what knights offered protection for Rosskinross.

"The knights of the manor and every able man have gone to join with the ceithern," she explained.

When they dismounted, an aged man, grey bearded and bent at the waist, took their horses toward the stable. Robert's armor and weapons and even Hicket's sword went with the horses, but Mila's karambit remained hidden under her tunic and she kept the orb in its box with her.

"Ceithern?" Hicket asked Maeve as they crossed the courtyard. "A word I have not heard before."

"You may call them kern. They are foot soldiers who have come together to fight to protect our land."

"Bands of kern formed to fight the armies of the lords who invade. Yes, I have heard of them," Robert said. "And yes, we know of the invaders intent to take possession of as much land as each can win and hold. Possession of the land enhances their standing here and increases their influence in England, makes them richer. It is a continuing invasion of this country, one begun under the reign of King John that still continues to this day."

Maeve's lovely face turned to another curious frown, as if something troubled her. "Begun under King John?" she said, as if this made little sense. But the thread of thought was not quite clear and its meaning escaped her. "Yes, your king encourages this," she said instead. "Though he may be at the head of it, this king of England, our real threat comes from the others, those of lower stature. The men who come into a manor, kill the family and any who stand with them, and then rule by force."

"Balian," Hicket murmured under his breath.

Maeve turned to him. "You know these foreign lords?"

Robert answered. "Only one. He sails to Wexford soon with many men, both knights and foot soldiers."

"But Wexford is far distant. You are nearer Cashel

and here our threat is immediate," Maeve went on. "Lord deRupe has led a band of men here and they have taken control of much of the land in the surrounding hills. He is a vicious man, cruel. It is his force that my father and brothers have gone to fight."

"deRupe," Robert repeated. "It is not a name I know."

"His force grows as he takes over more land. He parcels the land to lesser lords who then owe him allegiance. It is all done under the authority of your king John." Maeve fairly spat the name.

"Robert?" Hicket leaned toward him and grasped his arm. "Robert, she speaks John as our king. John is dead these many years."

But Robert discouraged Hicket's question with a warning glance. Instead of answering him, Robert reassured Maeve. "We are not with deRupe. We seek only a safe haven for a short time and promise to move on whenever you ask."

"Stay, then. We will offer you food and shelter in our hall, as is always the way at Rosskinross."

She led them through the great barred door that now stood ajar and into a hall that paled in comparison to that at Pynford or even Ricwyn. The air was not fresh, the walls were dark with soot and, if there were a fire at the center, it would have only a hole in the roof to vent its flame. "I will see to an evening meal," were her parting words as she left them in the company of a woman servant and several boisterous children who, showing a curious lack of interest, ignored the newcomers.

Mila wandered about the edges of the dim space, 'the hall of the manor of Maeve', examining every rough table and bench, chest and stool; but she was careful not to drift beyond hearing anything Robert and Hicket might say.

When they were alone, Hicket spoke first, anxious for an explanation. "Robert, we are but a half day's ride from Wexford. How is it that we are near Cashel?"

Robert lifted a finger to his lips to hush Hicket. He spoke softly. "And when my good mother, the Lady Emeline, came into the forest to meet with me, we knew she was absent from the manor for far too long, so long that we must devise a story to account for her absence. Do you remember?"

"I remember."

"Yet, when she returned to the garden the sun had not moved at all across the sky."

Hicket stared at his friend.

"There is more, Hicket. There is the time we spent traveling from Pynford to Ricwyn. That journey took far too little time."

"But can Wexford really be far distant?" Hicket frowned.

"It may be. I begin to believe much of the tale my mother told about the Orb that Mila conceals beneath her cloak."

Hicket continued to stare at him, struggling to understand the meaning of all this.

Robert spoke again. "In truth, all we can be certain of knowing is that this country suffers the invasions begun by John many years ago. The threat deRupe poses to Rosskinross is a result of the path King John chose and one that King Henry now continues to follow. Anglo-Norman lords invade this land with their armies, take over the manors and establish their own fiefdoms." Robert drew Hicket even closer. "I can see that it is a profitable business, one that would surely tempt the likes of Balian."

"He would increase the holdings of Ricwyn and of the higher lords who support his effort. And he would gain their favor. Yes, Robert, I see that this would profit Balian in many ways."

"If his effort is successful. If it is not, Ricwyn will suffer." Robert considered this, still at a loss to determine his own role in the scheme of things.

Hicket, though, took up another thought. "Landed barons aside, Robert, I think of what becomes of the peasants of the manors in this struggle?" He looked about the hall. "What becomes of these servants and the villagers and their children?" It was more statement than question. Hicket was concerned about the status of those in the same circumstances as his family, serfs who held land at the will of their lord.

Robert pondered the outcome. "It might benefit the newly established lords to create as little upheaval as possible among villeins. In that case, those who plough the fields and tend the kitchens might see little change."

But then his thoughts turned to the invasion. "In truth, little might change after the new lords take hold. But surely the peasants must be forced into battle in the cause of the present lord. All men suffer in war."

A woman appeared with a pitcher of ale and set it on a table before them and they were quiet in her presence.

"And the weakest suffer most," Hicket mused when she left them. "Surely the men who fight with the ceithern are now in grave danger, as are the unprotected women and children they left behind. There is no one here to defend the manor."

Robert's head bent forward as Hicket spoke; both were overtaken by a wealth of individual and common sorrows.

And then Maeve came to them from the back of the hall, from a door on the side of the kitchens. She walked softly, with a quiet grace Mila could never gain. From a short distance, Mila saw her face only as a pale oval, the luster of a new moon reflecting on an evening stream; and even in the dim light, her hair shown with the brightness of a gold coin.

Robert lifted his head as she approached and smiled at her, a smile she quickly returned.

Mila needed no owl to warn her that her idyll had shattered.

CHAPTER 29
The Plight of Rosskinross

Mila moved closer to the table as Robert pulled a stool forward for Maeve and placed it between him and Hicket. Born into the gentry of this land, Maeve sat gracefully and was immediately at ease with these two strangers, speaking their tongue with that lilting voice in soft words that carried only a short distance.

It was Hicket who soon noticed Mila clinging to a wall near them. "Mila, come join us. You have not spoken to Maeve."

Nor did she want to. But he gave her little choice, standing as he did, drawing a fourth stool forward. She pulled the stool a bit farther away than he had placed it and sat, albeit in a sulk.

Maeve was speaking of her family and their plight. And Robert! Robert was feasting on her words as if each were a priceless jewel. "deRupe is known about the countryside for his savagery. When we were warned that he and his force were besieging a neighboring holding, Neil Congalig, my father left to join the fight. Our knights and even the young squires and the men of the village are with him. My brothers had already left to join the ceithern; Damon has been lost and only the youngest survives. Our situation is desperate."

"And you are left alone here. Had they no thought to defend this manor?" Robert's voice was filled with concern.

"If they are successful in stopping deRupe at Neil Congalig, they will return. If they are not successful, it matters little. Alone, they would not be enough to stop deRupe. If they fail to stop him there, he will come here."

"What will you do?"

Her blue eyes lowered and she shrugged, a small, graceful gesture. "I regret we can do little. Lord deRupe is a cruel and powerful man. He will come here and take possession of our lands and we will suffer for it. Suffer even more than most I believe, because my family joined the fight against him."

Hicket, raised to be a knight from an early age, was appalled at the thought of harming the defenseless. "Surely he would not harm the old women, the children."

"Perhaps not. But they are loyal to us. I warn them against it, but they may try to harm him."

"And be punished for it," Hicket added.

All three sat in silence, as if awaiting a doomed fate.

But Mila was incensed by the weakness in Maeve. "So you sit here and wait for the worst to happen? Are you mad?" All three turned toward the girl they had all but forgotten. "I would do something."

She was met by stunned silence and her face burned, but she knew she was right in this. "Slip away while you might and live off the land until better times. Hide on the island or in the trees as you did when we came to this place and stay hidden until your enemy feels secure and leaves but a small force here to hold Rosskinross. Then attack. Or plan an attack as the force arrives and is ill prepared. Choose any path other than the weak one you have chosen."

"God's bones, Mila," Robert began.

But Hicket had developed more respect for the cunning Mila. "Mila may be right. Why must you sit here unprepared and wait for an enemy to come to you. Surely there is another way. Any choice is better than this."

Maeve was having none of it; she balked at the idea. "deRupe has a strong force. In truth, we are only women and children. We can do nothing."

"In truth, you can do little," Hicket half agreed. "But nothing?"

As he listened to Hicket's words, Robert, too, began to assess their plight. "Are there any men who may join you? Ceithern who may return here if they survive the fight at the neighboring manor?"

Maeve and Mila turned to him, but with different expressions. Maeve at last saw a glimmer of hope; but Mila was appalled. This was the simpering Maeve's trouble, not Robert's fight.

And then, in an instant, he made it his. "Have you any stores of arms remaining in the manor?" he asked.

"All the arms that remain are stored in the safe room behind the stables. Many, I fear, have gone with the men." She looked up at Robert and another smile brightened her face. "Come, I will show you."

"We can lend three horses, but only armor for one knight," Hicket said as they rose to follow Maeve.

Robert smiled. "But we are two knights."

Mila's face set into a scowl. So now it was Hicket's fight, too. She tramped behind the three in wonder. God's bones, they were all mad.

The store room, though, held more arms than any of them had foreseen. Rosskinross had expected the arrival of some part of the invasion force for several years, and they built up an armory over that time. The weapons were not the stuff of knights but the arms of foot soldiers: javelins and throwing spears that might pierce armor; knives, short and long, and light swords; slings; a few bows with quivers of arrows. There were stores of padded coats, but no mail, and only small helmets and shields.

Mila, who followed Robert and Hicket into the room, was amazed at the wealth of weapons, almost as much as she had discovered in the cellars at Ricwyn. She stalked about the room behind them, examining each different part of the collection.

"Arms but no soldiers," Maeve said at last.

"At least arms," Robert answered.

"Yes, at least arms," Hicket echoed. "But who will bear them?"

"How many people are left here?" Robert asked.

Maeve smiled at him, but it was a smile of futility. "Few men, only those too old to fight. The women, of course."

"All the women?"

"Yes, all the women of the manor and the cottages in the fields."

"Numbers?"

"The steward would know."

"The lovely Maeve would not," Mila said under her breath. "Not of interest to her."

Only Hicket was near enough to hear, and he frowned down at her. "Maeve would deal with the household, Mila, and have less interaction with the villagers. That is unfair."

But Mila just scrunched up her nose and shrugged at him.

"We should gather everyone together." Robert saw no real purpose in the plan, but he was unwilling to abandon any glimmer of hope he could give Maeve.

"We can do that." She looked up at him and her tone changed. "I can do that."

Robert was smiling as he watched her leave them.

Mila only said, "God's bones," and she was careful to say it quietly enough for Hicket not to hear.

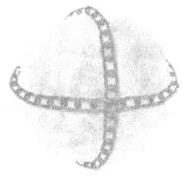

CHAPTER 30
Arms Without Men

Though Robert was transfixed, Hicket paid no heed to the departing Maeve. He was busy opening crates and examining the contents.

"More slings, Robert," he called, "sturdy staff slings of good length. These would be effective in the hands of any good shepherd, even a youth."

"There are shepherd boys here," Mila contributed. In spite of her misgivings, she found it impossible to ignore Hicket's growing enthusiasm. He looked up from his task to listen to her. "There must be. There are many sheep on the hill beyond the fields." She joined him in the task of opening crates.

As the door closed behind the departing Maeve, Robert finally turned to help them in their search of the storeroom. Together they gathered an impressive collection.

"We should sort the weapons and armor into some order," Hicket suggested. "Slings, swords, shields."

Mila surveyed the assortment. "We should also sort them by size." They both turned to her. "Look at this." She lifted a heavy javelin, barely able to hold it in both hands. "Now what would I do with this?"

She moved on to one of the smaller slings, two woven leather cords, one ending in a knot, one in a finger ring, and with a leather cradle at their center. She put the ring around her finger, grasped the knot in her fist and spun it around her head a few times. "If someone showed me how to aim, I could send a rock flying with this."

Hicket could picture her doing it well. At every opportunity, she had practiced slashing the air with her karambit until now the blade whipped back and forth in her hand, lethal with any upward or downward stroke. The image of Mila armed with the sling made him shudder.

Robert stood over a sturdy woven basket. "We have no need to use rocks." He held up something that to Mila looked like a duck egg, except that it was a bit more flattened into sharp edges and had points at both ends. "Look, we have a store of metal projectiles."

Hicket uncovered a similar basket nearby and found smaller metal balls. "Projectiles of different sizes."

And so they sorted: Javelins; knives; swords; shields; padded armor; slings and projectiles. Mila worked behind them, further sorting each type of weapon or armor into smaller groups by size: knives with long blades and heavy handles that were awkward in her small hand; short, light knives with slender blades that suited her well.

When they had opened most of the crates and baskets, Hicket walked along the piles of weapons. "We have no axes, Robert, no broad swords. In truth, nothing of weight. Those must have been taken by the men."

Mila scowled at the suggestion that this was a shortage. "Nor have we any use for them. Aside from you two, I see no one about who could swing a broad sword."

Robert did see the need. "Mila, you cannot face an enemy in hand to hand combat with a sling."

Aye, he was mad. She walked nearer to his side, looked up at his great height and the span of his shoulders. "As if I could face you or Hicket in hand to hand combat. What would I do with an ax, chop at your toes?"

At this, Hicket broke into gales of laughter, and despite himself, Robert joined in. No one noticed Maeve enter the room. She was standing there staring, not aware of the source of all this mirth.

Robert and Hicket were each quick to begin an apology, but it was Mila who stepped forward and explained. "We were considering how we might best use the weapons we have at hand with the people that remain."

Maeve saw no humor in this. She looked toward Robert seeking his thoughts, but it was Mila who had the idea. "We cannot stand against any force of men who come here, however large of small. Aside from Robert and Hicket, we are but old men and women and not strong enough for combat. Nor are we trained for it. But there might be another way. If our numbers are large enough and if we remain hidden and are able to use the weapons we have, we may turn them back."

Again Maeve's eyes searched Robert, but he stood transfixed in her gaze.

Hicket, though, again saw the sense of Mila's thought. "Perhaps," he said. "In this way we may have a chance, however slight."

Robert finally took up the idea. "You mean an unexpected ambush. Yes. At least we would be better prepared than if we do nothing."

It was all that Maeve had waited to hear. It was clear that if Robert thought an idea had some substance, she would follow. "I have gathered the women from the manor and the village. The priest remains with us and so we have seven men, though the others are old and of little strength."

"Is there a boy who tends the sheep? One who spends his days in the fields?" Mila asked.

Maeve frowned. It seemed such an odd question. "We have shepherd boys, yes."

"Many of the women will need to learn to use a sling, and shepherds will already be trained in this," Mila told her.

Maeve looked up to question Robert, just as Mila looked up at Hicket, shook her head and frowned.

But Hicket kept any reproof of Mila to himself. He realized it was natural for her to be scornful of the beautiful Maeve. Mila's inbred reaction to any dire situation would be so far beyond Maeve's imagination.

Robert moved to Maeve's side now, gently taking her elbow. "Come. Take us to those you have gathered. We will explain our thoughts and ask if they are willing."

"We'll explain our thoughts," Mila echoed under her breath, and again Hicket heard her. He grabbed her elbow to usher out through the stables and into the courtyard. "God's bones, Hicket," she asked him, "are we the only two who are not mad?"

CHAPTER 31
A Priest on the Path

The number gathered in the yard of the manor was as surprising as the stores of weapons. True there were few men, but the women of the village were of hardy, wiry stock, accustomed to heavy work in the fields. Even many of the women of the manor, those that scrubbed and carried, were young and strong. The children were either very young or girls, for even the youth had gone to join the fight against deRupe. The priest in his clerical robes was a tall, ungainly fellow; he stood at the front, heads above the others, with a few old men clustered about him.

Together, they were not a promising lot, but one common force united and fortified them: deRupe. They were all terrified of the man. When Maeve told them that God had sent them help in the form of these strong knights, Robert de Ricwyn and his companion Hicket, Mila could sense the feeling of hope that rose through the crowd. If they were given any chance to save themselves from life under the tyrant, they would grasp it. When Robert spoke, they fell silent, each straining to hear the champion that had been sent.

His message was short, as no exact plan had been formed, but he gave them the skeleton of Mila's idea: we are many; we have faith in our cause; and we are in possession of weapons that suit our abilities. If they learned to use these weapons well, they might set a trap for the unsuspecting deRupe. Coming from this towering, powerful knight, the words were inspiring.

Any plan coming from Mila would be less so, but they did need a plan.

Still, the first part was already determined. They would have to fight with weapons few had ever used. Hicket moved to Robert's side and asked, "Is there anyone here who can aim a projectile, draw a bow or throw a javelin?" Surprisingly, there were more than Mila thought possible. The many holy days the church declared, days of rest for the peasants of the field, were filled with games that required these skills. Hunting, too, was a common pursuit.

Hicket asked those with a particular skill to step forward. Some did this voluntarily; more were called out or even pushed.

"Avice is deadly with a sling. Taught her shepherd sons, she did."

"Margery, the butcher's wife, can wield a knife proper."

"Joan, where are you?" The crowd parted around a

tall, broad shouldered woman. "Joan can draw a bow as good as any man." Joan was reluctant. "Yes you can."

And so it went.

Hicket drew the skilled apart and led them to the store room to select a weapon that suited their strength and ability. "Now take a few more," he instructed, "those of the same type, and teach one or two others to use them. But be careful to gather back arrows and projectiles. We must use them again." It was an eager band he formed, energized by the thought of using anything against the hated deRupe.

Robert was more interested in the land they must defend, at first believing that planning an ambush might be an easy task. He believed that an unexpected attack on a band of invaders spread out along the steep, narrow path leading to the lake shore would have a chance of achieving some measure of success.

But when he asked her, Maeve explained that this was not the main approach to the manor. The cart path that led from the manor house to the cluster of small cottages of the village continued around the settlement, through the fields beyond and up over the eastern ridge to the main road. This was the route commonly used to reach Rosskinross.

Robert was eager to ride out along this path to survey the approach, and Mila rushed to join him. He asked the priest, a learned man long of the village who spoke both languages, to guide them. Maeve called the priest Cormac, so Robert followed suit.

Cormac had no horse and guided them along the path on foot. Once past the village, the path broadened, lined as it was with open fields, and then it ascended a slight rise to the main road. As they walked their horses along, they saw that the earth beneath them was beaten hard, firm and easy on the horses hooves, and that it was an open approach with few trees or bushes along the way. Robert realized that there was no place to conceal an ambush along the entire distance, even as Cormac assured him that deRupe would bring his force this way. Robert rode the short distance from the edge of the last field up the rise to the road several times, only growing more discouraged by the lack of prospect.

Mila had never seriously thought about the logistics of an ambush, but she remembered how they had been attacked in Pynford Forest and how they stopped the messenger from Ricwyn when they wanted a horse. "It would be trees that we need, Cormac," she told him as they watched Robert ascend the rise one last time. "A copse of trees would narrow the path of those that approach and also give us protection."

"We cannot grow trees in a day," was his only reply.

Mila thought of the Orb resting inside her tunic, but she had no idea how to capture its power over time. They would need to find a better solution.

At last Robert returned discouraged. "I see no place along here to halt a force and turn them away."

Cormac suggested the narrow paths that wended between the cottages. "If we could force deRupe to enter the village, we might attack him there. It is a place familiar to us, but not to him."

Robert looked toward the village. "Why would armed men approaching the manor house this way turn into the village? They would ride around the cottages to the manor gates."

It was Mila who approached this dilemma as she did all things. "If we cannot attack him here, then we must send deRupe to the better place, to the path we used when we came to Rosskinross. In truth, Cormac, it was the steepness and narrowness of that path gave us hope for the plan."

"But we cannot change his course. deRupe will come this way." Cormac was sure of it.

Mila rode ahead of the priest in his slow pace, and studied the path. "Not if this path is impassable," she said when she returned. "What would make it so?" She wasn't asking but thinking aloud.

"Boulders," Cormac suggested.

Robert scanned the hillside. There were many boulders up there, but they would be impossible to move within a short time and with so few men.

"Felled trees then," the priest went on. "But there are so few trees near this path. Fire? No, few trees, so nothing to burn."

"Water?" Mila smiled as she said it.

Robert gazed back toward the rise. "The land does dip slightly there, just before it ascends to the road. Still, even if the gully were filled with water, it would not make a very wide gap. Men would ride over it."

But Mila was looking in the other direction, toward the fields. "But what if the fields were flooded? There would be little way to ride around that." Her eyes searched the hillside. "See, they lie in low ground, Robert. And even if deRupe led his men to higher ground up where the slope begins in order to avoid the flooded fields, he would have to descend from that path into the village. And I agree that he would like to avoid the village."

Robert turned to look toward the village. "In that case he might decide to circle round and come down the path to the lake shore. But how could we flood the fields, Mila?"

"Oh we do it often," Cormac spoke up. "Aye. When the weather is dry and we need to wet the fields, we divert the stream." He led them back toward the village, explaining as they went. "That stream runs down the hillside and spills over the dam by the miller's cottage before it flows into the lake. When the steward and the tillers know the fields need water, we board the dam higher and the water flows into ditches that lead to the fields."

"And the path?" Robert asked.

"Well, the path, too, floods. An annoying but necessary consequence of sending the water in this direction."

So Mila was going to flood the fields. Robert smiled at her, then had a further thought. "To be prepared, we will set sentries to warn us of anyone approaching either path. Would you find a vantage point and be the first to watch here at the end of the fields, Cormac? Watch from somewhere you can see anyone who approaches the top of the rise? You could then give the hue and cry."

The priest agreed to find a place near the main path and even to wait there today until dark. As they left him to settle in the crook of a fruit tree, an owl hooted.

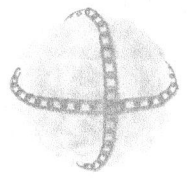

CHAPTER 32
Maeve Rises to the Challenge

When Robert and Mila returned to the manor, dusk was gathering. The meadows along the lakeshore were filled with small groups of women and children, the air filled with flying objects. They watched as Hicket walked among the groups selecting the most adept, moving those less promising on to different groups, and in his way making orders seem more like kindly suggestions. "Your aim is good, but the bow is too stiff for you to pull. Go there, try the stick sling." Or, "You are strong. Perhaps not a knife, but a spear." Hicket had secured the safety of his army, too, making certain they remained at a distance from each other and always aimed outward. This, though, made any approach to the meadow a lethal undertaking. Robert dodged several projectiles to move forward and wave to his friend.

But all were growing tired, so Hicket returned to the manor with Robert and Mila seeking provisions. They were surprised to find that Maeve had already had the younger children of the village bring stores to the manor kitchen; she had organized those too old or frail to handle weaponry to prepare a simple potage that they could carry back into the fields and village. When that was done, she joined the others at a table in the hall.

Robert stood to give her his seat, putting her in their midst. "Hicket tells me that you have an unexpectedly adept corps of warriors," he said as he sat beside her.

"Their skills are surprising," Hicket told her. "They would have no hope in hand to hand combat, but many have strength and good aim. And now Mila believes that we will be able to challenge deRupe in a place suited to their skills."

Maeve looked toward Robert. "You have found a suitable place on the cart path?"

"Not on the cart path but on the narrow path that descends to the lakeshore," he told her.

"It is suited for an ambush, we know that. But surely deRupe would not choose that approach." She raised a brow and at last turned her attention to Mila. "Why would he even attempt it?"

Mila refused to give an answer, so Hicket did in her place. "If the fields are flooded, he will be forced to come that way." Maeve's face brightened as he spoke and she imagined the cart path hidden beneath a sheet of water. "It was Mila's thought," he added.

At last she appraised the girl. "Yes, I can see it." There

was more in this urchin than she had expected. This time her lovely smile was for Mila.

Still, she turned to Robert for action. "We have had rain and the stream flows full. So, yes, the water from the stream will fill the fields and the path will be impassable to men on horseback. But we must do it now, for it takes a bit of time." She was already standing to leave when she had another thought. "Robert, if we can dig a trench across the path between the fields, a trench that a man on horseback could not see under the surface of the water, wouldn't that make the path impassable, even if the water in the fields is still shallow?"

Mila looked up at Maeve, appraising her in a new way. When pushed into action, this beauty might be as cunning as she was.

As Maeve spoke, Robert stood with her. But when Hicket and Mila stood to join them, Maeve placed her hands on Hicket's shoulders. "Rest," she said, and her glance took Mila into the command. "This is but the work of a few and is best done by those here who do it often. I will take Robert to the mill dam and he will tell them the plan. Those that know how will easily divert the stream. I will see to it that the other villagers hasten to dig a trench before the water becomes too deep." And they were gone.

"I will take Robert," Mila mimicked Maeve's soft voice.

Hicket watched them leave the hall and then turned to her. "Mila, surely you can see that Robert already has feelings for her."

Aye, she could see it, but she would never admit it. She refused to look at him.

He placed his hand over hers, but she drew hers away, so he walked into the courtyard leaving her there hunched over the table, sulking. He watched Robert and Maeve hurry through the gate near the kitchen garden. Few lanterns were lit in the courtyard so Robert held her arm, keeping her close and guiding her carefully in the dim light. They were speaking softly, words Hicket failed to hear; in truth, words the likes of which he would never hear.

There were no squires about to tend the horses, so he turned toward the stable with purpose.

Mila was still sulking when she thought, "He totally forgot about Cormac." She rose and went into the kitchen for food for the priest, coming away with fresh bread, cheese and a covered beaker of ale. Alone, she found her way to the fruit tree at the edge of the fields and called to him. "Cormac, you still up there?"

The leaves rustled and the priest slid down to the ground landing with a plop. Rising slowly he unwound his long, stiff limbs, twisting and stretching.

She held out the cloth. "Cheese, bread." And then the pitcher. "Ale."

He took the ale first.

"Anyone?" she asked.

"Aye, just now. A group of riders on the main road. Enough riders to carry torches against the dark. But they did not approach the cart path."

"So not scouts?"

"I think not. Too many for a scouting party." He stuffed a lump of bread into his mouth, bit off some cheese and followed it with another gulp of ale. "A good many torches. I could see their light when I was up in the tree." More ale. "Look. See the brightness beyond the ridge?"

Her eyes followed the direction of the path to the rim. "I see light against the sky, but it does not move. Have they stopped at the entrance to the path?"

"Near to it. Most likely too dark to attempt coming to the manor now."

Mila thought about that. Something was wrong. "I should think darkness would provide good cover to attack a band of women and children. If that is deRupe and his force, they have no fear of a close battle. They would have no reason to wait for light."

Cormac just looked at her and chewed.

"Wait here. If I call out to you, get Robert and Hicket and bring them to me."

"Are you going up there?" He understood the peril in that, but he did nothing to stop her.

CHAPTER 33
deRupe's Men Search the Main Road

Mila left Cormac at the fruit tree and crouched forward making as little sound as possible. The night was dark, but the path was hard and smooth, so that at first she moved quickly. As she neared the top of the ridge she slowed and sought a place where the low bushes along the main road grew heavy enough to hide her from view and soft grass along the edges might dampen her footfalls.

Torches were still burning on the road ahead and she could see several men standing about holding their horses steady. Three men in their midst were chattering on at each other, not arguing really, but sharing different ideas. They seemed uncertain about what they should do, as if they had no clear objective.

She crept closer, trying to understand their words and was in luck, for their language was her language.

"Aye, he did say to find those that escaped the fight at Neil Congalig. But should we only search here at

Rosskinross? Can we be certain they would all come here?" The words were clear, but now, from her position low to the earth and behind a clump of bushes, she could not see the man who spoke or make out which he was.

"The lord was from Rosskinross, so those who followed him must also be from here. They will return here." It was a second voice.

"Well the lord and his son will never return, so the others may disband. Melt into the hills as these folks do." This from the first one who had spoken.

The second man considered this for a short time and found a better argument. "Their womenfolk are here, their children. These men have seen the forces of deRupe, have heard his promise to kill everyone at Rosskinross as he did at Neil Congalig. No, they will return here, if only to gather their families and take them away."

The third man entered the discussion. "That is so. Surely they will fear the slaughter of their families." This man was young, his voice higher, softer.

"But they are men of these hills. They will not come by the road." This argument from the first man.

"The reason for us to stay by the road now is that from this place we can fan out to take the lay of the land in the morning. We cannot do that when it is dark." It was the second man who spoke, and now he paused. Mila imagined him scanning the roadside, judging if it offered a clearing large and safe enough to make camp, so she shrank farther into the bushes.

He must have judged it so, for he soon added, "I say we stop in this place until daybreak. When the sun rises we can search the countryside for any who escaped and at the same time assess the defenses of this manor of Rosskinross."

"Stop here, then, by the side of the road?" This from the young man, who seemed not pleased by the thought.

"It is the main road to Rosskinross. He will come this way. If we have already scouted the entrance to the manse and even found some of the men who escaped, he will be pleased. What more can we do in the dark?"

After more words, many she could not now hear, they seemed to settle on this plan and moved to organize the men, sharing their thoughts, giving orders. But Mila had heard enough. She slid backward, away from the road and the light of the torches. Soon she was back on the hard earth of the path and rushing toward Cormac. She had already formed her own plan and would trust the priest to tell the others.

As promised, he waited under the tree, sitting now, long legs spread straight before him in an effort to loosen muscles cramped by hours in a tree. His first words were, "deRupe? A fighting force?"

"deRupe's men, yes, but not his main force. Still, more than just scouts. As many men as the fingers of my hands."

Cormac rose at the news, his eyes searching the path near the road. "Will they come now?"

"They were sent to search for those that escaped the

fight at a place called Neil Congalig. They intend to scout the manse and search the byways, but they may not ride into the manor until the main force joins them. Still, the men in charge believe deRupe will come soon."

"So deRupe has not been defeated as we had hoped."

"No Cormac, I fear not. And there is more." He bent down to better hear her. "The men spoke of the lord of Rosskinross and his son."

His face drew close to hers to see her as best he could in the darkness.

"Cormac, they said the lord and his son will never return to Rosskinross."

He froze as he was for a moment, for just a breath, then straightened to his full height, turned away, was silent. Mila waited; he seemed unable to move. "Cormac, we must be ready."

He turned to her, but the face above her was in shadow and she could not read his reaction to this news.

Maeve said he was of the village, had lived his life here and been a part of the manor for many years. Still, this may not be his fight. He was, after all, a man of God and would be accepted as such by all, by friend or enemy of the manor. Helping the lords of Rosskinross fight an invader might be all well and good when their fortunes were uncertain, but now that their fate was sealed....

So no, she could not feel confident in him, could not let her new plan rest on the narrow shoulders of this priest. She would have to delay long enough to find Robert and tell him what she was going to do. And Robert, most certainly, would not agree to the plan. Still, she was determined. She would tell him—and then she would slip away to carry it out.

She asked Cormac to take her to the dam at the miller's cottage, the place where villagers diverted the stream into the fields. She hoped Robert would still be there, watching the flow as it turned, studying the swiftness of the water, judging the effect. She expected that he would not leave until he was certain of the result of this effort.

As she and Cormac hurried back along the path between the fields, they met women with spades digging a narrow but deep trench across its lowest point. One woman with a lantern hailed them as they passed, and in the reflection of the lantern's light, Mila could see the earth between the rows of late summer growth in the fields was already darker, soggy with water. At this rate, the flow might soon cover the approach and fill the trench.

But the rapidly rising water was suddenly her adversary. Mila could never make her way back to the main road through the rough land above the village, not in the dark night; she would have to come this way. She would have to hurry.

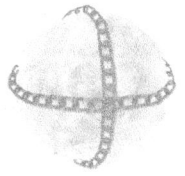

CHAPTER 34
Mila's Gambit

Robert was still at the dam beside the miller's cottage watching the water flow into the fields, but Maeve was nowhere to be seen.

"Mila." His spirits were high and he hailed her with a broad smile. "See this. The flow is swift."

She ran to his side. "It is. Cormac and I have just returned to the village by way of the cart path and we could see that the earth on both sides already grows soggy."

She turned to the priest who confirmed her words.

"Did you pass the women making a trench?" Robert asked.

She nodded. "They have chosen a place where the path is by nature low, so the water will easily conceal it. Any man on horseback who rides into it will surely lose his seat and pitch forward." She paused. "But Robert, I have news."

He studied her face and was alarmed. "Tell me."

189

She told her tale of the band of riders at the edge of the road, of their mission to search for men who escaped the battle with deRupe.

"So the fight ended in victory for deRupe. He has won that round." Robert was less spirited, but not as crestfallen as she had expected. "But here, Mila, we have a chance of defeating him. More, deRupe's men search for those who escaped. So those men will return here and join us."

"I fear they will be few, Robert, and will not include the lord of Rosskinross. Both he and his son have been lost."

This was the news that turned him. "Maeve's father and brother? Both?"

She nodded.

It took a moment for the news to alter his thoughts. "Both," he repeated. Then, at last, he formed another concern. "Mila, how could you know this?"

"They spoke in our language, Robert. They are from England."

"You spoke with them?"

"I was close enough to hear their words."

"Close." His eyes narrowed. "Mila, did you steal into their midst?"

"Only to the edge of the main road."

His face became a mask, no emotion turning his lips or creasing his brow.

Cormac chose this moment to leave them, slipping away toward the small village church. When he had gone

Mila touched Robert's arm seeking to regain his attention. "Robert, we have formed a plan of ambush. It is our only hope. We must act."

"Act. Yes. But first I must speak with Maeve. She must hear this news now. It may change the way she feels. She may decide it would be wiser for her to leave Rosskinross. Come."

He bolted toward the manor at a pace so brisk she had no way to keep even with him and fell behind. When she entered the manor hall through the great door, she found them there, Maeve and Robert huddled together near a fire at the center of the hall and Hicket standing over them. As she approached, it was Hicket who turned to her.

"Mila, you have brought this news?" It was a question. She nodded and he drew her aside. "Tell me."

So she was forced to repeat her tale a third time.

But unlike Cormac and Robert, Hicket's first concern was for her safety. His expression grew stern. "Mila, you took a great risk."

"It is very dark, Hicket. I was at a safe distance."

"You were foolish."

She hung her head, looked down at her new boots. Bullocks, they were muddied and badly scuffed!

Hicket shook his head, and again turned his attention to Robert and Maeve, who had suddenly grown quiet.

Robert looked up at him. "I cannot convince her to leave. She will stay at Rosskinross." He was not pleased with her decision.

Nor was Hicket. "It would be better to leave this place."

"It is my home, these are my people. I am responsible now," was all Maeve would say. So the decision was made.

Mila studied her again. She so envied this beautiful creature who stirred feelings in Robert that Mila would never own; this maiden who was so aloof that she must seek the exact numbers of her own peasants from a steward. But for all that, she would not leave Rosskinross and abandon them to an invader. There was more to her than Mila understood. Nor cared to. But the die was cast. Now it was up to Mila to secure the outcome.

She looked toward Hicket and realized that she could not share her plan with him. He would never allow it.

Perhaps Robert would stop her, too; tell her the idea was too dangerous.

She watched him console Maeve, cup the lovely pale face in his hand, stroke the gold red hair. No, it was certain: Robert would do anything to help Maeve. Mila was just a soldier in his force, expendable.

And she had to go now, before water covered the cart path.

"Robert." He was startled by Mila's call, as if he had been unaware of her presence. He turned to look at her. "I must speak with you." He was reluctant to leave Maeve, even for a short time; but Mila was insistent and he followed her to the door of the hall.

"Robert, deRupe's men camp near the place where the

cart path meets the main road. If I hurry, I can reach the place before the path floods."

"Mila! No! Why would you even think of returning to their camp?"

"I have a plan. If I were to stumble into their midst and give them a tale of running away from the manor, they would not have reason to doubt me."

His expression grew speculative.

"Robert, I am but a scullery, a slave in the kitchen, overworked and with no allegiance to my masters. In truth, I would be foolish to remain at Rosskinross if given a chance to escape."

"But what could you hope to accomplish from this, Mila? You could do nothing against so many men."

"I could mislead them, Robert. I could tell them that when the village women heard of the great victory of deRupe at Neil Congalig, they abandoned the land leaving only Maeve and her few maidservants in the manor. I could even show them the path that leads to the lakeshore, tell them to come in that way."

"Surely they will have to come that way now, Mila, with or without your advice."

"There are still two approaches to the manor. In the daylight, they may decide to come across the hillside and through what they believe is a village with no men. If all your defenses were set up on the lake path, there would be no way for you to shift from the path to the village; they are on opposite sides of the manor. More, these men are not certain when deRupe will bring his larger force here, only that he will come soon. If I could convince them that the manor is abandoned and that they can secure it at no cost, they may be persuaded to come at daybreak, invade the manor and then present deRupe with a token of their valor and loyalty."

"You mean they might decide to come here before deRupe brings his main force and take possession of Rosskinross for him. Yes, if they are eager for spoils, I can understand why they might do this."

"But instead, they would be lost. Then when deRupe does come he would have fewer men, Robert."

"Yes, fewer men with him and no way of knowing what happened to the men who he sent on before. He would not know the danger of the trench in the field or of an ambush on the narrow path." Robert was beginning to see the advantage in Mila's plan.

"If I can convince these men to come soon after daybreak, we will even have the chance to test our defenses before the main force arrives."

Robert saw this, too. "All well and good, Mila, but you will put yourself in grave danger. Are you willing to do that?"

"It would increase the odds in our favor." It would increase the odds in his favor, and that is all that mattered to her.

And Robert was already considering how it might be accomplished. "If you are to convince these men that the village is abandoned, there must be no fires in the cottages." He glanced back at Maeve and Hicket who sat near the fire in the hall.

"All must be silent, Robert. And you must be ready to strike at daybreak."

He turned away to stare out the door at the night sky and was quiet for some time considering—what? She had no idea. Finally he turned back to her. "No, Mila, it is far too dangerous. You must remain here." But his objection was in words only. There was no force behind it. His attention had already returned to Maeve.

So Robert would not call out to Hicket, who he knew would stop Mila from attempting so dangerous an exploit. As he crossed the hall back to Maeve's side, Mila slipped out the great door and into the night.

CHAPTER 35
Spinning a Web

Before she left the manor yard, Mila went into the kitchen garden and dug a small hole in a corner behind the rookery. She buried the orb along with her new boots and leather belt. Even though she took the time to do this, she was through the lakeside gate and halfway to the village when she heard Hicket calling her name, running after her.

He was too late, as Robert must have judged he would be. She bounded from the path, tumbling into the tall grass of the lakeside meadow, remaining silent until he passed; only then did she creep forward through the grasses along the lakeshore. She skirted the village and avoided the cart path, slogging instead through the fields which were now under a rising flow of water. By the time she reached the rise to the main road, she was covered in dirt, her new tunic and even her hair slimed with mud.

deRupe's men had stopped farther up the road, a

short distance away from the entrance to main path to the manor. They had settled in for the night with only one fire burning against the dark and chill and only one sentry standing watch. Mila moved toward him through the bushes at the roadside, making more noise as she drew nearer.

The man was alert. "I hear you," he shouted when she was quite near their fire. "I hear you there. Come out."

One of the others stood. "Who is it?"

"Someone there, in the bushes."

The second man came toward her and she stood. Mila recognized him as one of the men who decided to camp here, an older man who held some authority.

"Come out," he ordered again. When she did, he grabbed her by the shoulder and dragged her to the fire.

"But a ragged beggar," was the sentry's appraisal.

"No sir," she answered. "I am not a beggar but a servant in the manor of Rosskinross."

"A servant of the manor," the man with authority scowled. "Not the likes of you."

"I serve in the scullery."

"You are filthy. Even these people would not keep the likes of you."

Mila looked down at her new tunic and in the light of the fire saw for the first time the mud caked rag it had become. "I came through the fields. The fields and the path are flooded."

"Flooded?" the second man asked. "It is the wrong

time of year to flood a field."

Now a third man joined them.

"Who is this?" he asked.

When he spoke, Mila recognized him as one of the three who made the decision to camp here. She looked up at him. He was quite tall, but slimmer and more finely dressed than the other men, a long soft cloak pulled round against the night air. The others deferred to him, as if he were a man who held greater sway, so she decided to take charge and speak to him.

"I am Mila. I worked in the kitchens of Rosskinross, but now I leave there."

"You are running away from your master, then?" The thought of a servant running away displeased the young man.

"There are none to run from. They have all left the village. Even the manor stands empty but for the mistress and her few maidservants. It may be that now they have gone, too."

"Gone?" he repeated. "Gone where?"

"They would never tell the likes of me, would they?" She looked round at all three. They were listening. "A man came by earlier today with news, and they all left. All but the Lady Maeve."

"Left?" the younger man repeated her again.

She just said that. Was this fellow slow? "Took what they could and left." She decided to use the words the men had used earlier. "Melt away into the hills, isn't that what these people do?"

"What was the news this man brought to Rosskinross?" This from the man who had pulled her from the bushes. It was a better question than those from the young man.

"He spoke their language, so I could not know, could I?"

The young man obviously had not paid heed to their common language before and now was confused by it. He spoke again. "But you speak as we do? Why are you here at Rosskinross?"

"I came with my mistress and her other servants. My mistress came to teach these people to speak as we do." Mila was pleased with her explanation. It sounded possible.

The young man was pleased, too. "So those at Rosskinross speak as we do?"

God's bones, he was slow. "The family. Not those of the village."

All three fell silent, frowning. It was the second man, the one she heard make decisions, who finally chose a course of action. He spoke to the sentry. "Will, take another man and walk down that path. Go quietly. See if those fields are flooded."

"Aye." And Will was off.

"You," he said to Mila. "Sit here near the fire where I can see you."

And so they waited, the older man standing watch, the younger man pacing about the fire and unsettling the horses, Mila sitting as quietly as she could.

It did not take Will and his companion long to return with the news.

"Flooded."

"The fields and the cart path?"

"Both, and with water rising. We will not be able to ride that way, not for many days. More, we heard no voices and saw no fires in the village beyond the fields."

The older man scowled. "So we will not be able to judge the lay of the land surrounding the manor nor search the village for any who returned."

"My father will be furious," the young man said.

His father? Mila was astounded. Was this a son of deRupe?

He turned on her, raising a fist, and for the first time since she joined these men she was afraid. But the older man held his arm to deflect the blow.

"Leave her be, Estienne," he said. "She is not to blame. The people of the village did this to us. It both slows our progress and denies us their crops."

"Aye," agreed Will. "These people are a cunning lot."

The older man, though, saw the good in it. "But hear what the scullery says. Except for a few women, the manor is abandoned." He turned to the young man. "Your father will be pleased with that."

The news of the flooded fields, though, had angered the young Estienne deRupe, and now he had grown petulant. "He would be more pleased if we were in possession of it."

The older man was more sensible. "We can wait for

the fields to dry. Then the way to the manor will become passable."

Mila saw her chance in the impatient young man. She looked up from the fire. "The fields will not dry if the water is not turned back."

They all turned to her.

"They flood the fields by turning the stream," she said, and then shrugged as if it were of little concern to her. "As long as the stream is turned, the flow continues and the fields stay wet."

Estienne deRupe pondered this. "So we must stop this flow?"

"If you hope to ride to the manor on the main path you must return the stream to its natural course and allow the fields to dry."

Now the older man became concerned. "Where do the villagers turn the stream?"

"There is a dam within the village at the miller's cottage. They turn the water into ditches at the dam."

"And when we stop this flow, the fields will dry?" the young deRupe asked. "The path will be passable to riders?"

"Not for days. Many days." He did not like her answer. None of the men liked it. "More than that if the weather turns wet." They did not like this at all.

Mila took advantage of their displeasure. "Still, there are other ways into the manor. The high ground above the village is rough, but passable. And there is a second path that leads to the lake shore and directly into the manor."

At last the impatient young deRupe was pleased. "A second path?"

"Aye. I have seen men on horseback approach the manor that way."

He was excited by the prospect. "If we followed that path, would those remaining at the manor be taken by surprise?"

Not to appear too eager, Mila just shrugged again.

He turned to the older man. "If we approach the manor now, before they expect us, we few could secure it before my father arrives." He grew more zealous. "He would find us already in possession of Rosskinross." He said this as if it would prove a stellar outcome for him and for them.

Mila was excited, too, but she must do nothing to let them know this.

The older man was skeptical. "That was not our charge."

"But it is abandoned," Estienne argued. "We know that most of the men were lost. Now the others have fled."

Will agreed. "They would not flood their fields, ruin their crops, if they were hoping to live on here."

Mila could see the older man beginning to waver. He turned to her. "This other path that leads to the manor, is it truly suitable for horsemen?"

"It is narrow, but I have seen men on horses come that way. The path leads from the main road into a heavy wood, but it is a short distance." She lied well. "It soon opens on the shore of a lake and from there leads to a gate in the manor grounds."

"You can take us to it?" he asked.

"Of course I can, as I have seen people come that way before." She must not seem too eager. "Still, I do not wish to return to Rosskinross."

Now the young Estienne deRupe spoke up with haughty authority. "You will do as I say."

CHAPTER 36
An Owl and a Knight in Shining Armor

Soon after daybreak the older man, Darton they called him, organized the foray. They rode forward on the main road several abreast with Darton at the center of the front row and Estienne deRupe at the middle of the second. Mila was not certain if the young man was placed there in order to shield him or because he was not trusted in the lead.

It was Darton, too, who decided to put her up front, just next to him astride a large boned warhorse ridden by Will. Unlike the time she shared a horse with Hicket, though, these men did not trust her at Will's back; instead, they pushed her in front of him where she could see the path and where she might even prove an effective shield.

She led them along the main road a short distance to the point of the fork, the very same course she, Robert and Hicket had taken just the day before. But, no, it could not have been that day, for now the road was much different.

The junction of the wooded path was a barren spot:

there was no ramshackle cottage crumbling at the turning; no wheel spun, nor was there any sign of a man to spin it. More, as she thought back, she could not remember seeing the main cart path turning off this road; if they had come by yesterday, they could not have missed it. She was here now, but when was that?

And still, the road forked much as it did when she first came by, so she pointed to the wooded path and turned them toward Rosskinross.

As the path narrowed and grew steeper, the riders were forced to alter their formation, first riding two across and then in a single file. At this, Darton became uncomfortable, wary of having his force spread out along uneven ground and enclosed in a dense wood. Mila and Will were directly behind him, and he called back to her, "How much farther?"

"We come to the end soon," she assured him, though in truth the path was longer. "You will see the light on the water of the lake."

He turned to look forward, but saw only thickening gloom. Then a twig broke nearby and he was suddenly aware of the danger.

It was too late. The path had grown too narrow to even turn a horse well and far too steep to climb quickly. They could be trapped in this place; Darton wanted nothing so much as to see the end of it.

He slapped his horse. It bolted forward.

And fell. Someone had drawn a rope across the path, a

rope strong enough to trip a horse and rider.

Dalton flew forward, thrust over the head of the struggling animal. He landed hard against a rock, and then tumbled farther down the slope, his body ending in an unnatural twist.

Will called for the others to halt, but they could do little else as a loud shout rang out from behind the veil of trees and the air filled with the sounds of a battle.

The men were behind her so Mila could see little, but she could hear cries as arrows and javelins and missiles hit their targets.

Will tried to turn their horse, but the frightened beast refused. His thought, then was to hold Mila close, use her as protection, and move forward around Darton's horse and away from their unseen attackers. Again the horse refused, rearing instead, throwing them both to the ground. As they fell and rolled together, crashing into the roots of a large tree, his face contorted into a mask of anger and terror unlike anything she had ever seen. He grabbed her tunic, pulled a long knife from his belt and raised it to strike.

Will's black fury, though, caused a hesitation: a moment to spew venom, to curse her. It was an instant, only an instant. As Mila screamed an owl swooped down into Will's face blinding him with furious wings and striking talons.

Then Hicket was there, too, behind Will, raising his sword. Mila turned away and Will fell silent.

When she turned back, Hicket stood above her staring down at the unmoving Will; he withdrew his sword and sheathed it as if in a trance. Only then did he kneel to lift Mila from the ground and carry her deep into the safety of the wood.

She was aware of him then, holding her to him, stroking her matted hair the way Robert had caressed shimmering gold curls.

"Mila?"

She smiled up at him. Her chest ached where it had slammed into the tree, but she could move her arms and legs and her head was clear.

"Fine, Hicket. Fine."

He held her close for a moment. "God's bones, Mila. What made you take this chance?"

She had no answer, but he needed none. All between them was understood.

And she realized the wood had grown quiet.

"We must see to this," was all he said. He stood, pulling her up with him. A short distance away, the scene of the skirmish was both horrifying and, as the women emerged from the trees and heavy undergrowth, growing jubilant: a strange mixture of death and celebration. Robert was at the center of both.

He called out as they returned to the path. "No one escaped to the road, Hicket."

"All are here, then?" Hicket asked. He surveyed the path in both directions. "None escaped in either direction?"

"None, I tell you." He slapped Hicket's back. "We have prevailed."

Mila slipped away from them, pushing upward along the path amidst the confusion of frightened horses and women dazed by the success of their feat. She stopped only when she found the man she sought.

"Here," she called back to Robert and Hicket.

The crowded path erupted into cheers as the knights passed.

Mila stood over a young man, huddled and silent now, but still wrapped in his soft cloak as if the ground beneath him were cold. Cold it may be, here on this shaded path; but cold earth would no longer matter to him.

At last Mila turned away, looked up toward Hicket and then Robert. "He is Estienne, a son of deRupe."

Neither had to repeat the words 'a son of deRupe' to understand her meaning. The message altered their faces and their actions in an instant.

Robert stood tall. "Quickly, now!" he shouted. The victorious warriors fell silent. "We must clear the path. Move these men into the cover of the trees. Gather all weapons. Lead the horses to the manor."

Hicket had already turned to the task. He secured the reins of deRupe's horse and stilled it, then handed the animal to Mila to steady as he returned the young man to his saddle. The impatient young deRupe would ride across it now.

"We must get him to the manor, Mila. Is this something

you can do?"

She looked forward, judging the course in front of her, surveying as she did the quiet scene on the path. Jubilation had ceased when Robert spoke out and now the women only waited for guidance. All that remained was the carnage. "Yes, Hicket, I can."

He touched her face and then bent to the work that must be done.

On her way down the path toward the lakeshore she passed Robert, already gathering more horses. He looked up at her as she passed, but his face was tense. There was no smile on his lips.

"The owl," she thought, as she picked her way down the path. "Where is the owl?" She glanced upward, but if it guarded her progress from a perch in the tops of the trees, it was invisible and silent.

Cormac guarded the gate. He opened it when he saw Mila leading deRupe's horse toward the manor but secured it after her as soon as she entered the courtyard. Her appearance startled him.

"Mila?" He stared at her tunic.

She looked down and realized that it was stained with blood and, once again, she had to assure someone who cared that aside from some bruises, she was unscathed. As they spoke, Maeve opened the great door of the manor and ran into the yard.

"We heard the sounds of the clash. The cries." Her eyes

implored Mila to give her good news.

"Just now all is well."

"The others?"

"All are well. Not one has been lost. deRupe's men were scattered along the steep, narrow path when the attack came from all sides. It was unexpected, and the horsemen were trapped and sorely outnumbered. They could do nothing."

Maeve closed her eyes and sighed deeply at this, a relief from the tension of the past few hours.

"But there is more." Mila handed the reins of the horse to Cormac and walked to its side. "This man was with the others."

Maeve's eyes questioned her.

"He is the son of deRupe."

"Hugh? Is it Hugh?" Maeve's voice was filled with concern, a concern that Mila felt unjustified.

"I know him as Estienne."

Maeve let out a breath. "The younger son, then." She moved to Mila's side and raised a hand to touch the soft cloak. "deRupe will never forgive us this."

He would not. A truth they all understood. They stood in thought until Hicket banged at the gate.

Cormac flinched at the clatter, as if wakened from a trance, and ran to open it. It swung outward and Hicket led several horses into the yard. He was followed by the broad shouldered archer, Joan, who led even more. They were soon joined by the others leading horses or carrying weapons, hurrying through the business of clearing the path. deRupe would come soon, and now he would be searching for his son. Rosskinross would need to form another plan. There was little time to waste.

In fact, there was no time. deRupe had already come.

CHAPTER 37
DeRupe's Men Stumble

There was little reason for him to wait. As part of a systematic overtaking of the scattered manors in this part of Ireland, deRupe and his forces had besieged Neil Congalig. The small holding was poorly defended, as they found many in this land were, and he was merely awaiting them to surrender when the lord of Rosskinross arrived leading several of his own knights along with a group of wandering Ceithern.

Despite the surprise of their attack from their rear, deRupe was able to turn his disciplined band to face this new force and to defeat it. His losses, though, were greater than they would have been if they expected an assault and this angered him. Still, the result of the skirmish was that deRupe not only prevailed at Neil Congalig, but he had defeated the lord of Rosskinross. His victory over both manors was complete; he had only to seal their fate. What he saw as the treachery of the lord of Rosskinross made him eager to do so.

Few escaped the battlefield at Neil Congalig, certainly none from within the pale. When deRupe secured a manor, he killed all within; no need to deal with the questionable loyalties of the natives. His only task now was to find and punish any remnants of the men who came with the lord of Rosskinross, and he must do it quickly, before they disappeared into the hills to join with other bands of Ceithern. Those who lived on the neighboring manor would return there to gather their families first: it was their way. If he hoped to stop them, he must send his own men to Rosskinross quickly.

But who could he trust with this mission? When he surveyed his diminished ranks scattered about the courtyard of Neil Congalig, tired men sorting through weapons of the fallen or resting as best they could, he realized the high cost of this battle. Still, a contingent must be sent now. He made the decision.

"Darton." A grizzled old captain stood. "We must hunt down those who escaped."

Darton was weary, not pleased with the idea of another mission. But he had ridden with deRupe long before they left the shores of England and knew any protest was useless.

"Many will go to Rosskinross. Take Will and," deRupe paused, took stock of the men who were now staring back at him, "and ten more." He saw a group resting near the stable where horses had yet to be tended. He pointed to them. "Those over there. And take Estienne." His younger son was soft; it would do the boy good to ride hard after a battle. "Ride toward Rosskinross. Search the roadside, study the land and the approach and the manor, if you can. We will secure this Neil Congalig," he almost spat the grand, odd sounding name of this ancient manor, "and join you soon."

And he would. There was little left to do at Neil Congalig. He would sort out the land in time, but now only a few men were needed to guard the manor: all those within the pale were dead; the wretched peasants of the field were too frightened of him to rise up; and there were no others.

Even before daybreak, as was his custom, deRupe left Neil Congalig under the watch of almost as many men as Darton had taken and led the rest of his force up the main road to Rosskinross. The band was now smaller than it had ever been; as the sun rose in the sky, they traveled quickly.

They gained the head of the main cart path to Rosskinross just as the skirmish in the wood broke out. Shouts, then the crash of arms and cries rose from somewhere on the slope across the fields and beyond the village. deRupe pulled up to listen.

"There," the huge warrior shouted, drawing his double edged battle sword and pointing it toward the distant manor pale, the lakeshore and the steep, wooded slope beyond. "There."

He plunged down the cart path at a gallop, and his men followed. Some young, swift warriors flew past him in their headlong quest for glory. Down the gentle slope they thundered, down toward the flooded fields.

The beaten earth of the cart path offered hard, sure footing to the galloping horses and the tops of crops still rose above the sodden fields, so those in the lead paid little heed to a covering of shallow water. They spurred their chargers toward the sounds of battle at a murderous pace.

And fell: three men, then five, then more at their back. First the hidden ditch and then an unexpected pyramid of fallen men and horses took a toll.

deRupe was able to halt his charger at the water's edge and raise his hand to those still behind him desperately calling for them to halt. They looked on in stunned silence as the fallen struggled to stand, sort weapons, calm frightened horses. A few did not stand quickly; some of these never would. His elder son, Hugh deRupe, was among those who stood, but his horse floundered in the muddy water and Hugh was visibly shaken by his fall.

And still the sounds of battle called them.

deRupe shifted his attention away from the fallen men to again scan the landscape and was quick to choose his next course. Almost before he could point to the hill behind the village others were off, leaving the cart path and riding up the side of the slope to circle the waterlogged fields.

But here the rise grew steep, the earth uneven and rocky. Progress was slowed even more by a mountain stream that raced down the hillside toward the village. There was no way around it: no bridge across and no obvious ford. The course was not wide, but the bed was rocky, slippery, the water swift. Lazily grazing sheep lifted their heads to stare dumbly at the slow progress of swearing men and stumbling horses.

By the time they struggled to the edge of the deserted village, deRupe's force was a scattered lot. And more, now the slope that rose from the far side of the lake had grown quiet; no sounds of battle, no shouts or cries, drew them forward. One by one the men halted, a diminished cluster of tired warriors with no plan.

deRupe, though, wanted blood. He owned this manor of Rosskinross, land for his ego and legacy for his sons. He would punish its contentious people, those who dared think they were strong enough to fight him. He ordered his men to search through the quiet cottages for villagers. "They may have taken refuge in the church. If they did, we can bolt its door and burn it down."

But as they rode the narrow lanes between cottage gardens they found not one, not even a child or a village priest.

They gathered again at the other end of the village, the place where the main path from the manor forked to enter the cottage lanes or lead into the flooded fields. From here, deRupe could see his men and horses still struggling in the flood water where they had fallen. The lack of villagers to absorb his wrath further angered him. He raised his sword one more time and led his band toward the manor.

They rode along the edge of the lake meadow to the point where the path to the lakeside gate of the manor split from the path to the front gate. deRupe signaled for them to halt. He stilled his horse. Paused. Listened.

Insects, birds, rustling grasses. Was the manor as deserted as the village? Or was this another trap?

He knew there could be few men here. Most already had been lost. But what of the sounds of battle?

He called back into the troupe. "Hugh."

There was no answer.

He turned to search through the remaining members of his band and a man from the back of the pack called out. "Hugh is not with us. He was among the men who fell in the water. He has yet to rejoin us."

At this deRupe scowled, his mood growing ever darker. He turned back toward the manor. His eyes followed the path that led along the shore and into the wooded slope. "There are no signs of a recent skirmish here." He was voicing his thoughts and asking for the thoughts of others.

A man at his side said, "It was nearby."

Another called out, "Voices carry across water. It must have been up there." He pointed toward the rising wood across the bottom of the lake.

Their eyes followed, scanning the wooded hillside for signs of life. Or death. But the path disappeared under a dense growth of trees and the slope was silent.

The man at deRupe's side spoke again. "These people

are gone. If they tried to escape that way, Darton might have found them. He would stop them."

"Aye, that would account for the clash we heard. But where are they now?" deRupe wanted to know.

"The people? Dead most likely."

"No, fool!" deRupe was losing his temper. "Where are our men? What has become of Darton and Estienne? The others?"

A different concern rang out from a man at the back of the band. "The gates here are closed. They will be barred."

deRupe's attention turned back to the manor. Silent. Most likely deserted. He spoke to the man at his side. "Take some men. Circle the wall. See if there is any sign of people within."

After the battle sounds of the morning and the treachery of the flooded path, this man was unwilling to leave much to chance. He divided the band's remaining warriors as he saw fit, riding forward along the path to the main gate in the lead of several horsemen. deRupe either felt secure and paid no heed to the number leaving him or was too angry to calm down and question it. Either way, it was a mistake.

As he waited near the lakeside gate, his men disappeared around the corner of the pale, first turning onto the path toward the front gate and then leaving the path altogether to circle the manor. Near the path to the front gate the surrounding land was hardened by many years of travelers to the manor who wandered off the path or by visitors who camped there to wait for the gate to open to them; but as the horsemen rounded the next corner at the far side of the pale, the land under them retained its natural state: tall meadow grasses in places sprouting from soft marsh and bog.

Unlike the obvious protection of a cliff or a moat, lakeside bog was an unexpected manor defense; still, it was effective as it was not good ground for heavily armed horsemen. First one then another floundered, trying to find footing in the soft earth. From the main path at the other side of the manor, deRupe could not see their struggle, but others were watching.

CHAPTER 38
A Second Attack

They knew deRupe was there for some time; they heard the clamor as his men pitched headlong into the ditch. Then they watched from the top of the pale as those that escaped the ditch began to climb the hillside above the village.

There was little they could do. They could bolt the gates and mount the wall with their weapons. Here, Robert and Hicket could arrange them as they saw fit, a mix of heavier javelin throwers and those with lighter slings, spread apart enough to not hit each other—as well they might with most having such little experience. But they realized they had no hope of denying this many armed horsemen entrance to the manor. And once the men were inside, the women knew their fate in hand to hand combat was sealed.

But they had fared well on the wooded path. In truth, that fight was against a smaller band and conditions there were more favorable to their lighter weapons. Still, as they cleared the path, they had all considered a second flight into the trees where they might again separate deRupe's band into smaller groups and have a chance. Now, as they watched deRupe's main force struggle across the hillside, they decided among themselves that this would be the best course for them and told Robert of their decision.

So as deRupe and his band crossed the slope and scoured through the village, most of the defenders of Rosskinross slipped away through the front gate. Avoiding the path, they darted across the meadows alone or in pairs and disappeared into the wood, each carrying as many weapons as they could manage.

Maeve refused to take this route; she would stay at the manor. Robert refused to leave her and Hicket would not leave Robert. He tried to convince Mila to escape with the women, but she, too, refused to leave. She would stay with...

Mila suddenly found herself questioning her motives. She would stay with Robert, surely. But as Hicket begged her to go, she realized that perhaps it was Hicket she couldn't leave.

In the end, only Robert, Hicket and Mila along with Cormac and a scattering of grey beards watched from the top of the manor pale as deRupe gathered his men and started down the path from the village. They were heartened by the number of men deRupe had with him, for it was not as great as the horde they had expected. Early battles had taken a toll, the surprise attack at Neil

Congalig took many others, and today an ambush and a deep trench at Rosskinross had taken even more; a good number of deRupe's men were scattered under the trees beside the steep wooded path or piled together in a ditch in the flooded cart path through the fields.

The women who had left the manor and carried their weapons into the security of the wooded slope watched deRupe, too. Many were still hoping for the return of any men who might have escaped from the battle at Neil Congalig and they wanted to hold off leaving Rosskinross for as long as possible; they felt they could wait for a short time in the dense trees that protected the steep slope. From this higher ground they, too, saw deRupe leave the village and approach the manor.

When several horsemen broke away from the main group and left the path to circle the manor pale, it was the broad shouldered Joan who saw an opportunity. She called quietly to those hiding around her. "Look. Those fools are still on horseback and riding off the path into the bog."

They were. And they had ridden out of sight of deRupe and the men still on the path near the lakeside gate.

"If we circle through the trees," Joan whispered, "we can get close to them. Those of us with bows have a good chance of reaching them."

But now there were others who watched from the

safety of the steep, wooded slope.

A few village men from Rosskinross had escaped the carnage at Neil Congalig. Only a few, but foot soldiers— cranny, strong men. As they crept away from Neil Congalig taking cover in the heavy undergrowth at the edge of the road, these men had seen Darton and his band ride past, heading toward Rosskinross. When the band passed them, they melted farther into the countryside and traveled far afield during the night, hoping to avoid any other search parties deRupe might send.

Morning found them back near Rosskinross where they saw deRupe and his main force approaching the entrance to the cart path. They took this as a signal to quicken their pace, sensing that any danger was now ahead and not coming down the main road behind them. Soon they drew close enough to the top of the path to see flooded fields, several horsemen wallowing in mud and others climbing the hillside behind the village.

"The wood," one of the men called quietly, and as a body they turned toward the slope where the steep path led to the lakeside. They approached the path cautiously, expecting to find more of deRupe's men searching for them there, but the only men they found were far beyond searching for anyone. Instead, they were scattered beside the path concealed in the bushes and undergrowth: horsemen that would never ride again.

"What is this?" they asked each other, astounded. "What happened here?"

"What happened to their weapons?"

"What happened to their horses?"

"What?"

One of the men turned to look toward the manor and spied movement in the trees nearby. He called to the others. Pointed. "What?"

Then the village women were astounded, too. As if by some mystical timing beyond their control, a small group of men appeared at their back, men amazed to find a band of armed women hiding in trees.

Amazed but quick to adapt.

The men had drawn close enough to hear Joan's thought. "If we circle through the trees, we can get close to them. Those of us with bows have a good chance of reaching them." But then Joan turned and saw the men from Rosskinross moving into the trees behind her.

"God's bones, Joan," another woman whispered, unwilling to take a chance. And then she saw the men, too.

The village steward, bloodied and bedraggled, slipped in beside Joan and said, "But we can reach them. We can."

It was not the warfare Robert or Hicket had been trained to fight nor even a tactic deRupe encountered. It was another blind ambush, plain and simple. As the tree line along the edge of the meadow exploded with volley after volley of arrows and missiles, men on horses mired in boggy earth had little defense against the unseen attackers.

Robert and Hicket saw it happen and were quick to respond, running along the top of the pale to a secure place above the stables. Mila and Cormac delivered a stream of weapons up to them and soon a hail of spears rained down from the top of the pale. The attack on the men in the meadow became a crossfire.

Unable to control their horses, the horsemen had no defense. Suddenly aware of their plight they dismounted, but heavy weapons and layers of protective clothing slowed their ability to escape from the muddy ground. The men and women with bows or slings found they had no need to leave the safety of the wood to attack deRupe's struggling raiders.

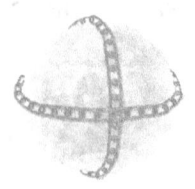

CHAPTER 39
Melee

For a second time that day, deRupe heard the clash of arms but could not see the battle. But this time he was closer and could take action.

He charged up the path toward the front gate of the manor and then off the path toward the corner of the pale. By the time he reached the point where he could see his men under attack, there was little he could do to help. The few who remained on horseback had all they could do to control their mounts. Those on the ground struggled through tall meadow grasses and boggy soil impeded by their hauberks or padded coats. None could respond to the attack.

deRupe turned to scan the tree line, measuring the distance and direction of the missiles. It was near, but to gain the position he and his men would also have to plunge into the meadow grasses. No.

The main path, though, led into this wooded slope. He

pointed to the path and his men swerved back toward the lake shore and from there along the path toward the trees. At the entrance to the wooded slope the path narrowed and the men were forced to form a single file.

The first entered the wood and began the climb into the dimness, but his progress slowed to a pace that angered deRupe.

"Move, move," he shouted.

The horseman tried to pick up speed at just the wrong time. Earlier in the day, after they had cleared the path as best they could, Hicket and Robert drew the rope back across it. So again a man fell.

deRupe watched from the lakeshore and was furious. "Ride! Ride!"

As he demanded the others push aside the fallen horseman and climb the path, one did, and then another. But as the path grew steeper, darker, nothing deRupe did could make them ascend faster.

Then a missile flew out from the dark undergrowth. And another. A second man fell from his horse and lay motionless on the ground, the horse rearing and losing its footing on the steep slope. deRupe pulled up. They could not hope to fight an unseen enemy hiding in a dark wood from a position on the steep path. This was a hopeless course.

At that moment the first man to fall called out from beside the path. "Darton!"

deRupe rode forward.

"Darton," he called again. "Here, by this rock."

The man who rode at deRupe's side swung down from his mount and climbed to examine the fallen Darton. He saw the wound to his head and the unnatural twist of is body. "Darton," he called back to deRupe. Then he looked upward along the undergrowth at the side of the path and saw more. "And Will." He pointed upward. "Will, there by the root of that tree."

"Estienne?" deRupe shouted.

Just then the trees erupted with missiles and the path became deadly. deRupe pulled back to the lake's edge and those not yet on the path fell back around him. The men bogged down in the meadow were lost to him, and now two more had joined the others strewn along the path.

deRupe seethed. He turned toward the manor pale calculating how many were left within. Few. It must be few.

He raised his sword. "Storm the gate."

He was too blinded by rage to see that his numbers were also few. Too few.

More, after the losses at Neil Congalig and the losses of this morning, not all were willing to follow him. As he galloped toward the manor some refused to ride with him and, instead, quietly retreated along the lakeshore; others slipped to the back of the charging band, rode to the point where the path toward the side gate forked from the main path and then rode away toward the village.

The gate deRupe charged was the lakeside gate near the kitchens at the far side of the courtyard from the stables.

Robert and Hicket continued their attack on the remaining horsemen who struggled to escape the meadow leaving the gate unguarded. Within moments one of deRupe's men had a rope up and over the pale and was inside. By the time Mila screamed a warning, he was able to lift the bar from the gate and the others stormed in.

Few, but still too many for Robert, Hicket and the man Mila realized was the faithful Cormac. At Mila's warning, Robert and Hicket shifted their assault from the meadow below to the men in the courtyard. From their vantage point at the top of the stables they were able to create chaos in the yard as powerful, well-aimed javelins struck with a force that pierced mail and threw men to the ground. But as the mounted men leapt from their horses with swords drawn, Mila knew their cause was lost.

Not so the men and women in the wood. They watched deRupe turn his band toward the manor, watched men slip away from the pack to ride along the lakeshore and disappear into the countryside, watched more give up and ride toward the village. They counted how few followed deRupe. When the gate of the manor was thrown open, they needed no shouts or battle cries to draw them forward. This was their home and their fight.

From the top of the pale behind the stable, Mila saw them coming out of the wood and down the path. As the men in the courtyard mounted the pale toward Robert and Hicket, outside the pale a small army ran forward with bows and slings.

This army might not prevail in hand to hand combat, but they had proven themselves in ambush. "Cormac," she shouted. "Look! Open the main gate! Get them up here on the pale. Go, go."

Ignored by the fighting men, the priest in his brown robes ran round the pale and down to the front gate, throwing it open. Mila, too, ran but in the opposite direction, behind the manor house and down to the lakeside gate.

"Up," she shouted to men and women running down the path. She pointed them to the top of the pale. "Up there."

There was no time for concealment or careful placement. Men and women, too, rushed to the walk at the top of the pale, took aim into the chaos in the yard and fired. Arrows and missiles flew through the air into the courtyard and toward men climbing to the top of the stable.

deRupe cried out for his men to fight, but with what? Swords, battle axes, knives? Useless unless they could mount the pale. Some tried, some even made it. More did not. Many saw the opened gates and, fleeing from the fringes of the struggle, escaped.

Robert saw men riding away and feared deRupe might choose this path, too. He drew his sword and fought his way down into the courtyard, Hicket at his back.

deRupe saw them coming, powerful warriors swinging

their swords through the melee, purposeful and focused. Sensing their goal, he dismounted, raised his own battle sword and rushed forward, his loud curdling cry rising above the din.

Robert was ready, legs apart, feet shoulder wide, body balanced to deliver a powerful blow. As he poised his sword to swing, two men came at Hicket, one from each side. Hicket could only see to one side and thrust in that direction. Robert spun round, drew his arms in and slashed his sword at the second man knocking him to the ground.

As he turned back, leaning forward and again seeking balance, deRupe ran at him with his sword at waist level. Robert was able to twist away to avoid the direct force of the blow, but the sword caught his side cutting through his light armor.

The force of his lunge now left deRupe off balance. Robert was quick to take advantage, swinging his sword upward, knocking deRupe back; the upward thrust, though, made him aware of the pain in his side, the weakness of his arm.

deRupe, struggling to regain his posture, staggered backward toward the front steps of the manor. Robert pressed up the few steps after him, swinging his battle sword in broad strokes with all the strength that remained in him. deRupe's retreat was stopped by the great door; he leaned his back into it to gain leverage and prepared to thrust forward.

But the door, once locked in defense against the melee in the courtyard, gave way and deRupe plunged backward into the darkness of the hall. Robert hesitated for a heartbeat, wary of stepping into the dim light.

And then there was no need to follow, to plunge his sword downward into the warrior. deRupe lay prostrate before him, prostrate and still, a motionless heap crumbled on the cold floor, his eyes unseeing, his thick neck open and bleeding.

Mila stood inside, at the edge of the doorframe, her karambit clenched tightly in her hand.

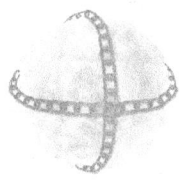

CHAPTER 40
The Fate of Rosskinross

Hugh deRupe, weary, wet to the bone and weakened by a huge gash across his forehead, carefully led two other horsemen along the path between the fields in water that almost reached their horses stirrups. As they struggled toward the village, the sounds of another clash of arms drew them forward.

But it was short-lived. As they reached the path to the manor they met men already retreating from the skirmish. Their accounts of the ambushes at Rosskinross varied, but all told tales of frustration and fear. And, try as he might, the young deRupe was unable to turn any of them back. Quite the opposite, for instead, the two men with him soon joined the retreat. When he rode down the path from the village, Hugh deRupe rode alone.

As he drew near the manor, two men charged through the lakeside gate and thundered down the path toward him. These were men Hugh knew well, men of the battle hardened inner circle closest to his father. They were the last to leave the manor and their news of the fallen was the hardest to hear; both his father and his brother were lost. They convinced Hugh of the foolishness of riding into the manor of Rosskinross alone and he turned to ride away with them.

As he turned away, those watching from the top of the pale cheered, but their celebration was short-lived, for within the manor courtyard there was little joy. There, too, it was a time of sorrow and loss and mourning. More, as they grieved, they knew that any success they had this day was not a final victory.

In time the villagers returned to their cottages and their work in the fields, toiling now to save sodden crops. Under the watchful eyes of Maeve and Cormac Robert healed, slowly regaining his strength. And as Mila studied Maeve to learn the gentle ways of the mistress of the manor, Hicket watched both young women mature and grow in wisdom.

Left unspoken was the acceptance of their plight: Rosskinross had endured a skirmish amidst an overwhelming invasion, but they could never win the war. At this manor, though, there would be no final battle. Neither side had the heart for it.

Hugh deRupe realized that the fault for his father's defeat lay in a series of hasty, foolhardy decisions made while fighting against strength that came from a unity of purpose. In truth, he could take possession of Rosskinross at any time: the army he could raise from his fiefdoms would be an undefeatable force and more, the power of the English king was behind him. But he realized, too, that though he suffered the loss of his father and his brother, his was not the only suffering. Those at Rosskinross had suffered, too.

If his father had been greedy for land and the power it brought to his family, Hugh deRupe was cut from a different cloth, and more, his was a new generation. Hugh had lived most of his life in this land; his aspirations were not in England, as his father's had been, but here among these people. Rosskinross, its land and village and the lake beside it, would be a valuable holding for him, but to hold it Hugh would not destroy its beautiful mistress and the people of her manor. In the end, he would find a more agreeable solution.

As is still common in this land of lakes and legend, in the thirteenth century folklore abounded. Troubadours of the Anglo-Norman invasion captured this tradition, promising the people of Ireland deliverance in the form of a powerful liberator, one who would appear from nowhere and free them from the foreign yoke. And, in truth, the liberator had come.

Much more subtle than a knight leading a powerful army, this liberator needed only time to steer a course away from warfare. During that time, the Anglo-French invaders became part of the fabric of the Irish nation, intermingled and indistinguishable from the people who had lived in the land before.

In that time, the lovely Maeve of Rosskinross was married to the powerful Anglo-Norman Lord Hugh deRupe. Together they combined fortunes to establish a new agricultural fiefdom scattered far and wide across the land and to found a family that would become one of the most prosperous of Irish baronies.

IRELAND IN THE REIGN OF
KING HENRY III

CHAPTER 41
Time

Time, under the influence of the Orb, followed many paths. Was it days or weeks? Memory fades.

One morning, as the sun crept over the manor pale, they knew it was time to leave this place and follow their true purpose. Robert must seek the forces of Balian; he must find Roland and help this brother as he might. Hicket and Mila were part of this venture and must go with him. The Orb would go with them, too. And, yes, an owl.

Robert might promise to return to Rosskinross, but when? Time was mutable. If Maeve asked him when, what could he answer? Only, "In the future."

As the mighty Abatos, the swift Alduin and Mila's steady mount, Luagor, climbed to the top of the wooded path and reached the fork in the main road, they came across a ramshackle dwelling near the turning. As he had before, a man in the foreyard worked on a large, wooden handled scythe, sharpening the blade on a stone wheel that spun unevenly.

Robert and Hicket approached him but did not dismount.

"Aye, they would not have you then?" the man asked, not looking up or even slowing his wheel. "They are a haughty lot, those deRupe's of Rosskinross. Even the cottagers of their village hold themselves above those of the nearby manors, though all the manors around here serve the same lord."

"All serve deRupe?" Hicket asked.

"He is a powerful man and his is a mighty family. Their land spreads far in all directions." He bent his back further into his work ending any more conversation.

They moved on then, riding east, eventually traveling along the river that descended into the harbor town of Wexford. Once again they were forced to circle away from Carrick Castle on the south bank of the river just west of the town. The Anglo-Norman stronghold ringed with a broad and deep defensive ditch spoke of the determination and power of invaders, and Robert knew that it would provide a haven for Balian's forces. They would be wise to avoid it.

Today Wexford was different from the sunny market town they remembered: the streets were dark under darker skies, the wind was up and the atmosphere somber. When they stopped at a stall for provisions, Robert questioned the man in charge and he answered in low tones in the language Mila had yet to fully understand. As they spoke Robert's eyes turned to the harbor, his attention growing more and more fixed on the activity around one of the boats moored there. The mast tilted to one side and the hull was damaged.

Mila could see his demeanor change, sense his concern. "Hicket, what raises Robert's concern? What has happened?"

"A storm, Mila. A storm blew in from the ocean to the south and brought with it a strong surge in the waves of this sea. It was unexpected. Many ships were pushed north, far off course. One crashed against the rocks of an island near the North Channel." His tone was grim. "The men aboard are lost. If any survived, they would be taken by the Norse who inhabit the island. Either way, they will not return."

Now Mila's attention followed Robert's. "The ship in the harbor?" she asked Hicket.

"It sailed with the ship that was lost but was fortunate to escape the waves." Hicket looked toward Robert as he answered her. "Both ships sailed from Newport."

Mila understood. "Balian's force was gathering there."

Hicket nodded. "Roland was with them."

"If these are the forces from Ricwyn, Robert would be known to many of them." Mila understood his dilemma. "I will go down to ask."

Before Hicket could grab her arm, stop her, she was off, running the short distance to the harbor. Unwilling to venture near the boat, Robert and Hicket were forced to stand idly by and watch her push through the crowded quayside, moving quickly from one man to another, tugging on their tunics and studying their faces as they spoke to her. When she bounded onto the planking that connected the moored hulk to the shore and disappeared among the men on deck, Hicket wanted to run after her, but Robert held him back.

"Let her be, Hicket. They will not pay her any great heed."

It was true, for within a short time she reappeared, this time leading a disheveled figure down the planking, a small man soon lost among the curious host gathered onshore. At last the two broke free from the crowd at the quayside and she was leading the man back to them. He was Roland de Ricwyn.

"Robert. Robert." It was all Roland could manage as he clasped his brother to his chest. "Robert." And after a time, the query: "Robert?"

In the midst of the busy market, people around them fell back and watched as the towering knight embraced a smaller, tattered fellow who had come from the damaged ship.

An old crone of a woman watching said, "I know that knight. He is Robert de Ricwyn."

Soon a larger crowd gathered around, buzzing like the bees of a summer field. "Robert de Ricwyn? It cannot be."

"Impossible."

"It is, I tell you."

"It must be his son then. Aye. The son of the knight of legend."

Others picked up the tale. "He is a son of the Robert de Ricwyn of legend."

But the woman insisted. "No, I was there. I know him. It is Sir Robert de Ricwyn I tell you, the knight who singlehandedly defeated the forces of old deRupe and made possible the union of his surviving son with the daughter of Rosskinross."

So, in one version or another, the exploits of the legendary Robert de Ricwyn were repeated once again. Fortunately much of the language spoken around her was still foreign to Mila, for she would have had much to tell them about the truth of the tale of singlehanded valor.

Robert parted the crowd and led Roland, Hicket and Mila away, escaping back into the anonymity of the countryside where Roland was able to tell them what had occurred.

When his brother, Lord Balian, gathered the stories of the messenger who lost his horse on the road south, the messenger who returned to Ricwyn from Pynford, and then those of his servants who saw Mila at Ricwyn, he realized that Robert must have been there. His immediate fear was that Robert had learned of his plans and had gone on ahead to Ireland where he would join with Roland and take over the invading force.

In light of these fears, Balian decided that he, himself, as Lord of Ricwyn, must travel with the Ricwyn forces; and more, these forces must leave immediately. So Balian and his invading army followed close on Robert's departure, dividing the force into different ships to sail across the sea to Wexford. When a storm blew in from the south and Balian's ship was lost, the invasion was doomed.

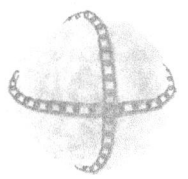

EPILOG

RICWYN IN THE REIGN OF KING HENRY III

In time tempered by the Orb, Roland and Robert were able to return to Ricwyn and make peace with Gregory of Pynford and other surrounding lords. It is now Roland's manor to hold, but both brothers choose to remain here.

Living in this familiar landscape of his youth, Robert sometimes fully sees his own impetuous past—the specter of an impulsive young warrior astride a massive charger forging headlong into the unknown. In these times, it seems well to call out to him, to urge the unseasoned knight to hold up, turn in his path and alter the future. At times Robert even tries.

At other times Robert accepts his fate. He sits at a window looking down at the people in the courtyard of Ricwyn manor: at Hicket and Hicket's eldest child, another Robert, dueling with wooden swords; at Mila resting in the sun toying with an embroidery hoop, her younger daughter Gwyndolyn and Roland's daughter Martha sitting beside her, an owl resting on a limb above them. At these times, Robert feels all was for the best.

But then, on the far side of the wall in Ricwyn's new knight's court, visible to Robert only when her faded hair and wan face appear between barrels and water troughs, Hicket and Mila's elder daughter sneaks toward the stable. She is another Emeline, a gentle name chosen to honor Robert's mother. It is a heritage ill-suited to the crafty child: this Emeline is up to something—again—something that most likely will result in upheaval.

This Emeline is too much like her own mother: incorrigible. Still, she is fortunate enough to have a loving family to embrace her and a mother to teach her that thievery is wrong.

Or might be. Perhaps Mila, herself, has never been quite convinced.

The manor and village at Ricwyn is a peaceful settlement on the farthest edges of Europe. Well to the east, Mongols invade lands and destroy civilizations, but that is another place. The European world builds cathedrals and founds universities and the English king and his great lords continue to cede power to men elected by shires and cities. It is a good time for men like Roland and Hicket and Robert.

They live together as each had always hoped to live: enjoying the fruits of their labor and, in every sense, having enough. Roland stewards the land; Hicket studies and writes; Mila is content with a home where she and Hicket are able to raise their children.

Robert, the legendary knight of Ricwyn, is heralded across the land in the songs and poems of troubadours. If fact gives question to his exploits, who is to expose the fact? Robert is content to be a legend. A legend and a myth.

HISTORY

England in the 13th Century was a spread of green forest and wide marsh, a land teeming with game and wild-fowl and festooned with wild roses and hawthorn. Spread across the land, small clusters of cottages clung to the walls of manor houses, monasteries or the occasional castle, with sustaining fields surrounding each settlement in a pattern that was repeated every few miles.

Society was stratified, mired in feudal dependence; but of necessity it was also one of individual independence insured by connecting roads which were often only rutted lanes, sinking deep into mud in winter and collapsing into dust in summer. Thus, the story of the expansion of the English colony in Ireland in the 13th century is made up of the actions of individual lords and knights with only occasional input from a distant King.

From the time of the Conquest in 1066, France became a semi-detached part of England, its language the language of the ruling class. Ireland was a land foreign to the English. An English gentleman would easily travel to

France as a matter of course but to Ireland only if forced by circumstance. In Anglo-French society, rich landless men could recruit armies and conquer Irish land for their King in the hope that the King would reward them by making them lord of the same land they conquered. This was often a way men could move upward in society, and it was the motivation behind much of the English invasion of Ireland. It might be seen as a form of expansion by privatized warfare.

In the Irish lands that had been secured by the Anglo-French invaders, an extensive process of colonization took place. Agricultural estates were formed and market towns were established to sell their goods locally, nationally and within Europe. English, French, Welsh and Belgians arrived to settle the lands of the new Anglo-French lords, while the Irish remained as serfs working on the estates. For most poor Irish this was largely academic: there wasn't a noticeable change in their daily of life. But things were different for the old Irish aristocracy: very few were able to retain their status and lifestyle.

HISTORICAL LOCATIONS
IN THE TEXT

Thomond, Offa's Dyke, Wales, Caerleon, Newport, Wexford, Carrick Castle and the Isle of Man are described much as historians believe they were in the 13th century. The channels, the currents, and the weather in the Irish Sea along with the hulks and cogs that sailed it are also factual. Pynford, Ricwyn, Rosskinross and Neil Congalig are fictional.

MathWord Press

www.mathwordpress.com

Teaching Mathematics through Literature
www.mathwordpress.com